The Happy Hollisters and the Mystery of the Totem Faces

BY JERRY WEST

Illustrated by Helen S. Hamilton

GARDEN CITY, N.Y.

Doubleday & Company, Inc.

Contents

CHAPTER 1

MUD-BALL TRICKS

"Help! Come quick!" Sue Hollister cried to her older brothers and sisters. "They're throwing mud at the wooden faces!"

Dark-haired Sue, who was only four, pedaled her tricycle furiously into the driveway of her home. Hearing her cry, two boys dashed around the corner of the big white house.

"What's the matter, Sis?" demanded the older one, named Pete. He was a handsome twelve-year-old with a blond crew cut and a friendly smile.

"Joey and Will are hitting the pole with mud balls and spoiling all the faces. Please do something!" Sue begged.

The other boy, seven-year-old Ricky, who had tousled red hair and freckles all over his face, asked, "Is this for real? Or are you spoofing?"

"No. Honest," Sue insisted, turning her tricycle around and starting to pedal. "I'll show you!"

"Where are Joey and Will doing this?" Pete asked, mystified, as he and Ricky ran after her.

"On Mr. Tompkin's lawn."

Inside the Hollister house, two girls had heard the

5

"Make those mean boys stop!"

commotion and rushed outside. The taller one, Pam Hollister, had fluffy golden hair and a sweet face. She and her six-year-old sister Holly ran down the steps. The younger girl's flying pigtails and impish grin stamped her as the family tomboy.

"Wait for us!" Pam called. Together the children, who had just finished eating supper, followed Sue down the street and around the corner.

Suddenly they saw a strange sight. In the center of the Tompkins' broad lawn stood a thick wooden pole about six feet tall. It was carved with curious-looking animal faces and topped by a bear's head. The figures, brightly painted in red, blue, green, and yellow, were smudged with blobs of mud.

"Make those mean boys stop!" Sue demanded, pointing.

Standing at the curb with a carton of mud balls were two boys Pete's age, Joey Brill and Will Willson. Right now they were looking defiantly toward the door of the house, where a gray-haired man waved his arms angrily.

"Go away!" cried the man, whom the Hollisters had never seen before. "Leave my totem pole alone!"

Joey smirked. Taking aim with another mud ball, he slung it. *Splat!* It hit the bear's head.

"Bull's eye!" Will cried, roaring with laughter.

Pete ran up to Joey, his fists clenched. "The man says 'Stop,' so why don't you?"

The bully glared. "Oh, butting in again? You stay out of this!"

7

Joey had teamed with Will Willson more than once to annoy the Hollisters and other persons in the neighborhood.

"Yes!" Will chimed in. "We don't want that totem in Shoreham. It's an Indian idol and will bring us bad luck."

"It's nothing of the kind," the old man spoke up. "Totem poles aren't idols, and as for this one, I carved it myself. Now go away and stop pestering me!"

Instead, Joey picked up another mud ball. "Try and make me!" he muttered.

Pete, furious at the boy's rudeness, backed up a few steps. "If you throw that, you'll be sorry!" he said firmly.

"Think I'm afraid to?"

"Go ahead," Will egged his pal on. "Hit Pete with it!"

Joey swung back his arm and hurled the mud ball. Pete ducked. The brown blob missed him, but hit Pam on the shoulder.

"Oh!" she cried as the mud ran down her dress. "You're a mean boy!"

Pete had had enough. He lunged for Joey. The bully, taken aback, turned and fled. Will was at his heels, followed closely by Pete.

"Get 'em!" Ricky cried as he dashed behind the trio. The redhead, however, stopped just long enough to pick up one of the mud balls himself.

Pete's fury made him run faster than the two bullies. He caught up to Joey, and with a flying tackle brought him down on a grassy strip between the curb and the sidewalk.

Rolling Joey over, Pete pinned his shoulders to the ground and sat on his chest.

"Say you're sorry!" Pete demanded.

By this time Ricky had caught up and stood over the two, enjoying the scene. He held the mud ball over Joey's head.

"How would you like to be painted up with this?" he asked with a grin.

"Don't—don't let him drop it on me!" Joey begged as he struggled to rise.

The move threw Pete off balance. He bumped into Ricky's arm. The mud ball fell squarely into Joey's face!

Enraged, the bully gasped and sputtered. "I'll get even with you for this!" he cried out as Pete let him up. "I'll get that old totem pole and I'll——"

Muttering threats, Joey and Will hurried off. Pete and Ricky, chuckling, returned to the Tompkins' lawn. The old man was helping Pam wipe the mud off her dress with a damp cloth.

"These are my brothers," Pam said. "Pete and Ricky, this is Mr. Roebuck."

As the boys exchanged handshakes with him, Mr. Roebuck said, "Just call me Old Ben. That's what everyone back home does."

He thanked the Hollisters for having saved his totem pole from further damage.

"Glad to help you," said Pete. "By the way, my

9

brother got Joey muddied up a bit—an accident, of course."

"He deserved it!" Holly burst out.

Mr. Roebuck's wrinkled face broke into a broad smile, setting off a twinkle in his gray eyes. "Boys will be boys. Well, I suppose you're wondering what I'm doing here with a totem pole."

He explained that Mrs. Tompkin was his great-niece. "I just came to Shoreham this June to live with her and her husband," he said. "They're on vacation now. I set up my totem pole as a surprise when they return."

"Did you come from Indian-land?" Sue asked him. She was still astride her tricycle.

"You might call it that," Old Ben said. "Alaska was my home for fifty years. I'm an old sourdough."

"But you don't look sour," Holly told him.

Mr. Roebuck chuckled. He explained that a sourdough was the name given to explorers and gold miners in the far north of Canada and Alaska.

"That's because we used to eat sour dough biscuits," the elderly man said.

He told the children that a small amount of sour dough was always carried by the old time adventurers. When mixed with bread dough, it acted as a leaven, making the bread rise before baking.

"It might not sound good to you," Old Ben said, "but when you're hungry it tastes mighty fine."

By now dusk was beginning to settle over the town of Shoreham and Pam thought the Hollisters should go home. But Ricky begged to hear more about the totem.

"I carved it as a hobby," Mr. Roebuck said, "and it stood in front of my little house in Juneau. But I brought the totem along to remind me of my happy days in Alaska."

"What is it like in Alaska?" Holly asked. "Is it fun to live there?"

Mr. Roebuck declared that Alaska, though most of it was wild and mysterious, was a beautiful territory. "It's full of dangerous brown bears," Old Ben added. "If you should ever go there, don't stray too far into the woods or you may meet one."

Pete then asked what a totem meant. The sourdough said that it was much like heraldry in England, or a family coat of arms. "The Indians read it from top to bottom," he went on, "and learned things about a clan or a chief's family."

While Pete helped Mr. Roebuck wipe the mud from his totem, the sourdough told the children that the bear on top represented a certain Indian clan. "They adopted me many years ago—as an honorary member," he said, smiling. "The chief was grateful because I had rescued his young nephew from a bear."

Directly beneath the bear on the totem was a salmon, and right under the fish was the figure of a man seated on an owl and holding a shovel in his hands.

"That's my old friend Emmet Gallagher," Ben Roebuck explained. "I made the wise old owl hold

11

him up because I think that Emmet is one of the wisest men in Alaska."

"How interesting!" said Pam, and Holly added, "Please tell us more about totem poles."

"Glad to," the old man said. "A very mysterious totem pole was lost somewhere in Alaska. The one who finds it will be lucky."

The Hollisters were eager to hear more. But because he was tired and it was growing dark, Old Ben suggested, "Come back again sometime and I'll tell you more about the mystery."

The children said good-by and set off for their home on the shore of Pine Lake.

Five minutes later they dashed into the Hollister living room, with all of them talking at once about Mr. Roebuck.

Their parents listened eagerly. Mr. Hollister was a tall, handsome, athletic man. He ran *The Trading Post* in Shoreham, a combination hardware, toy, and sporting goods shop. His wife was a slender, pretty woman with blond hair.

"It looks to me as if you've made an interesting new friend," she remarked.

"And the totem pole mystery," Mr. Hollister said, laughing, "sounds as if it might be spooky."

"Maybe we can find out more about it in the morning," Ricky remarked hopefully. "School's over for the summer."

Next morning the entire family was up early. Breakfast was barely finished when the telephone rang.

Pam ran into the hall to answer it. "Oh, no!" she exclaimed, then added, "Yes! We'll be right over!"

"What happened?" Pete asked as the others crowded around their sister.

"It's terrible!" Pam replied. "Old Ben's totem pole is missing!"

CHAPTER 2

THE ISLAND SEARCH

PAM hurried to tell her mother about Old Ben's misfortune.

"What a shame!" Mrs. Hollister said sympathetically.

"I think Joey did it," Ricky spoke up hotly, "just to get even!"

"We mustn't jump to conclusions," their mother advised.

"But we've got to help Old Ben!" Pete said.

"Of course, you must," Mrs. Hollister agreed. She said that all but Sue might go to his house. "Sue and I have a shampoo date."

"Please find the nice wooden bear face," the little girl called out as the others hurried off toward the Tompkins' house.

On the way they met Dave Mead. He was a good-looking, dark-haired boy Pete's age and often played with the Hollisters.

"What's the rush?" Dave asked as he pulled his bicycle up to the curb.

"The totem pole is missing!" Pete said. As Dave rode along beside him, he explained.

"I'll help you find it," Dave volunteered.

"Good, we may need you."

Arriving at the Tompkins' house, the Hollisters found Mr. Roebuck standing on the lawn looking sadly down into the hole from which the pole had been removed.

"We're sorry, Old Ben," said Pam. "And we're here to help you."

"Thanks. I don't know why anybody would play such a mean trick."

After Pete had introduced Dave, he said, "We think those two fellows who were throwing mud last night might have done it."

Old Ben sighed. "It took me nearly three months to carve that totem. I hope you can find it for me."

Pam asked him if he had telephoned the police. Mr. Roebuck said no. "It's probably just a prank. I don't want to get those boys into serious trouble."

Pam was impressed by the old man's kindness. She, too, always wanted to be nice to people and liked to solve mysteries without hurting anybody.

Dave spoke up. "If anyone can find your totem pole, Mr. Roebuck, the Hollisters can. They're great detectives."

Old Ben's face brightened at hearing this, and Ricky said, "We'll get to work right away."

The sourdough wished the children luck, then went into the house.

The Hollisters and Dave quickly mapped out a plan. Pete and Pam would go to Joey Brill's house and question him. At the same time, Dave, Holly, and Ricky were to make inquiries at Will's home. Then all would meet in the Hollisters' yard in half an hour and exchange news.

Pete and Pam hurried off down the street, turned the corner, and in a few minutes came to Joey's. Pete walked up the front steps and rang the doorbell. Mrs. Brill answered.

"Is Joey at home?" Pete asked.

Mrs. Brill said no. Joey had risen early, prepared his own breakfast, and left the house before his parents had awakened.

"Maybe he went fishing," Mrs. Brill suggested. She said good-by and closed the door.

In a low voice Pete said to his sister, "So Joey's gone fishing, eh? Fishing with a totem pole is my guess."

"Where do you suppose he took it?" Pam asked as she and Pete went down the walk beside the Brills' front lawn.

Suddenly Pete pointed at the ground. "Look, Pam! What do you think of this?"

There was a long gouge in the grass.

"It looks as if something heavy was dragged across it," Pam replied.

"Like a totem pole?" Pete guessed. "Joey dragged it this far and then somebody helped him cart it farther away."

"I wonder what Ricky and Holly and Dave found out?" Pam said as she and Pete hurried back to their own house.

Presently they saw the other children running toward them, waving their hands. "Joey and Will have gone off together," Dave reported.

While asking questions at Will Willson's house, the three had learned that the two boys had driven off in Will's motorboat.

Pete snapped his fingers. "That's it!" he exclaimed. "They're pulling the totem pole out into Pine Lake."

"Oh dear!" Pam said fearfully. "Suppose they set it adrift. We'll never find it."

"Let's chase them," Ricky suggested, "before they get too far."

"Okay," Pete said. "Suppose we take two outboard motorboats."

"Mine and yours!" Dave said. "Good idea. I'll meet you at your dock, Pete."

It was agreed that Pete and Ricky would man the Hollisters' boat. Pam and Holly would go with Dave in his. Pete called to his mother, telling her where they were going.

"Good luck," Mrs. Hollister said. "I hope you find the totem pole. But please try to stay out of trouble."

Pete promised. Then he and Ricky ran down the Hollisters' driveway past their rambling home and across the rear lawn to the shore of Pine Lake. The outboard motorboat was tied to the dock. Ricky jumped in first, then Pete, who started the motor and grasped the tiller. The craft purred out into beautiful Pine Lake.

Dave Mead's dock was close by, and Pete waved

The totem pole maybe?

to his oncoming chum. In two minutes the boats were riding side by side, their motors churning up wakes of greenish-white foam. Far out in the lake the children could see Blackberry Island, where they often went for picnics.

It was agreed that Pete and Ricky would search the south end of the lake for Joey and Will, while Dave, Pam, and Holly cruised northward. "We'll meet off the shore of Blackberry Island," Pete added.

He and Dave speeded their motors and headed in opposite directions. For the next forty minutes they went in and out of coves where Joey and Will might be hiding. They crisscrossed both ends of the large lake, keeping a sharp lookout for the brightly colored totem pole. But neither Will's boat nor the elusive totem came into view.

"I don't see how we missed them," Pete told Ricky and they shaded their eyes to scan the sparkling lake.

"I guess they slipped by us somehow," Ricky agreed.

Pete nodded as he turned the rudder and headed toward the place where they were to meet the others.

"Give her the gun, Pete!" Ricky cried out.

He stood in the bow, which knifed through the water, arching a spray on either side. The breeze riffled Ricky's hair and he narrowed his eyes to keep a keener lookout.

Suddenly he yelled, "Pete, starboard rudder!"

But the motor was making so much noise that Pete could not make out his brother's command.

Thud!

The boat shuddered as it bounced over a submerged object. Pete slowed the motor. "What did we hit, Rick?"

"It looks like a log! The totem pole maybe!"

Pete turned the boat about and headed for the log, which floated low in the water. At the same time he looked down at the aluminum bottom for any damage. There was only a slight dent. The craft had not been punctured.

"A lucky break," Ricky said in relief. As they drew alongside the log, he reached out and rolled it over. "Piece of an old telephone pole, Pete," the redhead announced, disappointed. "It isn't the totem after all."

"Well, let's tow the log to shore so no one else will ram into it," Pete suggested.

"Okay. But look! Here come the others." Dave's boat was streaking toward them at high speed.

When it came within hailing distance Pete cried out, "Did you see Joey and Will?"

"We think they're on Blackberry Island," Dave called. "Pam saw smoke coming from a fire."

"If that's where they're hiding," Pete said, "we'll find them pronto."

After telling about their narrow escape, Ricky pulled the log to the side of the boat and towed it toward shore. Nearing the beach, Ricky released the log to let it drift in.

Dave's boat was now in the lead. Pete followed him

along the shore of the island. A few minutes later Pam motioned toward a plume of smoke among the trees.

Both skippers throttled down their motors. As they neared the area of the fire, they thought that the smoke appeared to be coming from behind some bushes a distance from the shore. Pam signaled to Dave to guide the boat through a stand of tall cattails.

"There's Will's boat!" Holly whispered.

Pete and Dave stopped their motors. Then removing shoes and socks, they stepped into the water and pulled their boats up side by side onto the pebbly beach. The others leaped out.

Then the boys put their shoes back on and the searchers started off. They bent low as they crept toward the bonfire.

"Sssh! Don't make any noise, Ricky!" Pete warned as his brother stepped on a twig which snapped.

The younger boy nodded, then suddenly exclaimed, "Pete, look out!"

CHAPTER 3

ANGRY WASPS

PETE flattened himself against the ground. Ricky's warning had come just in time, for a stone whizzing over Pete's head plopped into the water behind him.

"Will Willson threw it!" Ricky cried out. "I saw him!"

He pointed to a movement in the bushes ahead of them. Will's head was just visible as he raced out of sight in the direction of the bonfire.

Pete and Dave dashed forward instantly. Pam called, "Be careful! Will may throw more stones at us!"

She said they should separate and approach the fire slowly from different directions. The boys agreed and the group spread out. Cautiously they crept toward the spot where Will had disappeared. All at once half a dozen stones were pitched toward them one right after the other, but the missiles dropped harmlessly among the trees.

"Good," Pete whispered. "They can't see us."

Holly, crawling on the ground, was soon out of sight. She worked her way forward like an eel, and was first into the clearing from which the smoke was rising. In the center was a bonfire, and poked into the embers were several long cattails. Not far away was a huge rock. Joey and Will were crouched behind it.

"Here they are!" Holly called out to her companions.

"Get away from here!" Joey growled. "Come on, Will! You know what we said we'd do!"

The two boys dashed up to the fire and each pulled out two cattails. Brandishing the fiery brown-tipped stalks, they jumped toward Holly.

"Don't you dare burn me!" she cried out, stamping her foot.

Suddenly Pete's voice sounded clear and strong. "Drop those!"

Joey and Will wheeled about to see Pete dashing toward them. Behind him were Dave Mead, Pam, and Ricky.

Joey and Will dropped the smoldering cattails to the ground. "No fair," Will whined. "We're outnumbered."

Pete said he and the others had no intention of hurting anybody. "All we want is the totem pole. Where is it?"

Holly gazed at the bonfire and blurted, "Did you burn it up?"

The bullies exchanged quick glances, and Will said, "Yes, we burned it up. Didn't we, Joey?"

Dave doubted that the pole could have been burned so fast. "Did you chop it up first?" he asked, noticing only small pieces of wood in the fire.

"That's right," Joey said.

"Then where's the ax?" Pete asked.

Pam noticed that Will kept casting nervous glances into the wooded part of the island. "You're fibbing!" she burst out. "You didn't burn the totem at all. You've hidden it."

"If you think so," Joey said with a sneer, "suppose you find it."

"Don't worry. We will," said Ricky as he started to walk among the tall trees.

Joey and Will did not seem to care. They apparently were too relieved that Pete and Dave were not going to fight them. Chuckling, the bullies hurried toward their boat. Pete followed to make sure they did not tinker with the two outboards.

"Oh, we won't touch your old tubs," Joey said as he and his pal started their motor and set off across the lake.

By the time Pete returned to Dave and Ricky, the girls had separated from the boys and were pressing deep into the woodland.

"That totem must be here somewhere and not too far away," Pam reasoned.

They looked right and left among the trees and bushes, until they came upon a rotted stump. Just for fun Holly kicked it. Part of the stump crumbled, and from it swarmed a horde of angry wasps.

"Run!" Pam cried.

Together the two girls dashed deeper into the

woods, flinging their hands over their heads to drive off the insects.

"Ouch!" Holly cried, and clapped a hand to the back of her left leg. "I'm stung!"

"Oh dear," Pam said. "That must have been the last wasp to give up the chase."

She bent down to examine the red welt on Holly's leg. Gently she found the stinger and pulled it out. "Mud will help it. Let's find some."

The sisters searched about until Pam located a damp spot where a jack-in-the-pulpit was growing. Using a twig, she pushed back a piece of moss and dug up a chunk of soggy earth beneath it. She pressed this against the injured skin.

"Feel better, honey?"

"Yes. Is that why the wasp bit me?"

"What do you mean?"

"You said I was honey." Holly grinned. "I'm all right now. Let's go, Pam, we have to find the totem pole."

The two girls made crisscross trails in the woods, staying within the bounds where they thought Joey and Will might have dragged the pole. They could hear Dave and their brothers searching a short distance away.

Pam stopped and called out, "Boys, did you find anything?"

"Not yet. How about you?"

Pam reported they were still looking, too. Just then

Holly called to her, "Pam, I think I see another log on the ground."

"Don't kick it," her sister warned.

The girls approached the log cautiously. It was covered with vines. Some of them seemed freshly pulled.

Holly reached down to remove them, but Pam grabbed her by the arm. "Stop! That's poison ivy!"

Holly grinned. "Thanks, Pam. You saved me from the itches."

Pam called to the boys and they ran to the spot where the girls were standing. They started to clear away the poison ivy with long sticks.

Bright colors showed through!

"Yikes!" Ricky cried out. "It's Old Ben's totem. See the bear's head?"

"Yes, and the old sourdough with his shovel!" Pete added.

Just then Holly burst out, "Say, do you know what's going to happen?" Before anyone could ask she added, "Joey and Will are going to break out with poison ivy!"

The others nodded. But Pam, feeling sorry for the bullies, said, "What a punishment!"

Because the children had no rope to tow the totem pole behind the boat, Dave had a suggestion. "We can lay it across our two boats," he said, "and carry it home that way."

"Good idea," Pam agreed.

Making sure that all the posion ivy was cleared from the carved faces, the boys carried Old Ben's totem

"It's Old Ben's totem!"

pole to the beach. Meanwhile, Pam and Holly ran ahead and jumped into their boat.

When the boys arrived, they took off their shoes, waded in, and laid the totem pole over the two boats. The bear's head rested on the bow of the Hollisters' craft. To the right of it, the base of the pole lay on Dave's boat. While Holly and Ricky held the ends in place, Pete and Dave started the motors, and the children set off toward Shoreham.

"Won't Joey and Will be surprised?" Ricky grinned as the boats zipped along.

"I wonder if they've started scratching yet?" Holly said.

Pete did not answer. He was concerned about the weather. The sun had been blotted out and dark clouds scudded across the sky. The wind had freshened, making white caps on the lake.

"A storm's coming," Dave called out uneasily above the sound of the rising wind.

As the boats continued their journey, the wind whistled louder. Larger waves sprang up around the boats and sloshed against the gunwales.

Pete looked worried. "Dave," he called, "we're lying pretty low in the water. Think we'll be able to make it?"

"Keep your fingers crossed, pal!"

Pam looked fearfully at the choppy water. The wave tips now were splashing into the bottom of the boat.

"Let's slow down our motors," Pete shouted.

29

"Okay."

But even at reduced speed, the boats were slapped hard and waves kept lapping over the sides.

"I guess we'll have to toss the totem overboard!" Dave cried out.

Just then a wave, higher than the others, caused the boats to dip crazily.

CHAPTER 4

THE KITTEN TOTEM

HOLLY cried out in alarm as the boat pitched wildly in the lake waters. At the same time the end of the totem pole rolled backward, pinching Ricky's finger.

The boy winced with pain but bravely did not utter a sound. Instead he grasped the pole firmly as his brother Pete ordered, "Hang on to it, Rick! I think the wind is dying down."

Pete was right. The strong breeze abated. But in its place a driving rain fell in sheets, pouring more water into the boats.

Dave and Pete realized instantly that they were now running into more trouble. They exchanged worried glances through the torrent, but said nothing as they did not want to alarm the younger children.

"We'd better bail!" Pete advised.

As Pam helped to steady the totem, Ricky and Holly scooped water out of the bottom of the boats with their hands. The children worked furiously, yet they were unable to cope with the deluge. The water now was deep in the bottom of the boats.

"Ricky! Holly! Put on your life jackets!" Pete ordered.

Both boats carried three orange-colored jackets which were tucked away beneath the seats. As the younger children reached for them, Pam noticed a large boat coming through the curtain of rain.

"Look, Pete!"

"The police launch!"

"Hurray, hurray!" cried Ricky and Holly. "We'll be saved."

Soon the throbbing of the police boat's powerful motors could be heard across the storm-swept lake. The large craft edged up to the motorboats and sheltered them on its lee side. Three officers made up the crew.

"Get aboard!" one of them called out.

Another said, "What's that log you have there?"

"A totem pole," Dave answered. "We're trying to save it!"

The policeman quickly pulled Holly and Ricky aboard. Then Pam was helped over the railing. The totem pole came next.

One of the officers gave two hand pumps to Pete and Dave. They bailed the water out of their boats. Then both smaller craft were tied to the back of the police launch. The two boys hopped aboard the launch and all started for the shore.

The police officers introduced themselves as Finch, Neary, and Smith.

"Your friend Officer Cal radioed us," said Officer Neary. "Your mother notified him that you children were on the lake when the storm began. She was worried about you."

"Now we'll let her know you're safe," Officer Smith said, smiling. He stepped into the little cabin and called the Shoreham Headquarters to get in touch with the Hollisters and Meads.

"Thank you," said Pam.

Ten minutes later the launch pulled up to the police dock at Shoreham, half a mile from where the Hollisters lived. The storm was nearly over, with dark, low-hanging clouds scudding away before a fresh wind.

Officer Cal was on hand to meet the children. He was a handsome, friendly young policeman who had helped the Hollisters solve their first mystery shortly after they had moved to Shoreham.

"Hi, ho, me hearties!" Officer Cal said gaily. "Good to see you safe."

"We didn't think we'd make it." Pete grinned ruefully.

After the children had thanked the officers, Cal volunteered to take the totem pole back to Mr. Roebuck. He added, "I think you can pilot your motorboats home now. What do you say, Neary?"

"Okay, Cal. But we'll stand by just in case your young friends need help."

Holly and Pam climbed into Dave's boat. Ricky joined Pete. They started the motors and headed back toward the Hollister dock. The police launch hovered behind them, then turned back as the two boats reached their destination.

Pam and Holly stepped out of Dave's craft and the dark-haired boy continued on. Mrs. Hollister ran from the house and greeted her sons and daughters with hugs and kisses.

Damp from head to foot, the children walked along the path toward the house. As they reached the kitchen door, laughter came from within.

"Sue must be having a lot of fun," Pam remarked. "I wonder what she's up to."

They found their sister sitting on the kitchen floor with her friend Donna Martin. Donna, seven, had dark hair and a deep dimple in each cheek. Scattered around the two girls was a collection of old shoe boxes.

In addition, Sue held White Nose, the family cat, in her lap. White Nose's five kittens were crawling over the two girls.

Snowball was perched on Sue's right shoulder while Tutti-Frutti's tiny claws clung to the back of the little girl's dress.

"Oh, you're tickling me!" Sue cried out, as the coal-black kitten Midnight pressed her nose near the little girl's left ear. Smoky and Cuddly purred quietly in Donna's arms. "I just love them," she said.

"What are you playing, Sue?" her mother asked.

"We're making a pussy-cat totem."

"Yikes!" said Ricky. "A totem with live cats?"

"Sure," Donna spoke up. "It's easy."

34

Picking up a pair of scissors from the floor, Sue said the girls would cut holes in the ends of the shoe boxes. "Then we'll stick the cats' heads through them, and pile one box on top of the other."

Pete smiled. "That'll be a neat trick if you can get the kittens to stop squirming."

"Oh, we will!" Donna remarked confidently.

It did not take the girls long to cut holes in the shoe boxes. As the others watched, grinning, Sue and Donna put the wriggling kittens inside and pushed their heads through the openings, making certain not to hurt the little animals.

"I'll take care of White Nose," Ricky volunteered.

The mother cat completely filled one box. She did not take kindly to having her head thrust through the hole. But White Nose was a patient cat. She had often been used in games by the Hollister children and had grown used to their playful ideas.

The five kittens, however, seemed to be less understanding. Their purring changed to tiny mews of protest.

"Here, hold still," Sue begged Tutti-Frutti. "We're not going to hurt you. This will be fun."

"You'll be the only pussy-cat totem in Shoreham!" Donna remarked as she kept Midnight from jumping out of the box.

Pete chuckled. "I'd say the only pussy-cat totem in the world—that is, if you can really make it."

The two girls held the kittens in place, and Ricky put White Nose in her box on top of the stack.

Now it looked something like a totem, but what a squirmy one! The kittens continued their mewing and kept turning their heads from side to side. Holly laughed when they stuck out their little pink tongues. Finally the two girls took their hands off the boxes. They stood back for an instant.

"There's our pussy-cat totem!" Sue giggled. "Isn't it cute?"

"Oh yes!" said Mrs. Hollister.

The children laughed gleefully. Just then they heard a low bark from the living room. A beautiful collie dog bounded into the kitchen.

"Quiet, Zip!" Pete ordered.

The family's pet dog usually was very obedient. But the strange sight of the kittens in the shoe boxes caused him to yip loudly. This frightened White Nose and her brood. As cat and kittens leaped in every direction at once, the boxes fell this way and that.

"There goes the totem!" Pam said. "Too bad, Sue and Donna."

In two seconds the cat family had vacated the shoe boxes. They dashed down the cellar steps to the safety of the cool basement.

As Pete helped pick up the cardboard boxes, he said, "We have some work with a real totem pole. I think we should get into dry clothes, then go over to Old Ben's and help him put up his totem."

Mrs. Hollister readily assented. "You certainly are doing your good deed for today," she told the children, smiling.

"There go the pussy cats!"

"Oh, we can do lots of good deeds," Ricky remarked cheerfully. "Besides, if we help Mr. Roebuck some more maybe he'll tell us about the mysterious totem pole in Alaska."

Leaving Sue to play with Donna, the four older children quickly changed their clothes and hurried to the Tompkins' house. The totem pole lay on the front lawn and Old Ben was busily shoveling loose earth from the bottom of the hole.

"Wait! We'll help you," Pete offered as the children ran up to him.

As Pete took the spade from the man's hands, Old Ben said, "I can't thank you enough for finding this. Good work, children!"

The Hollisters grinned, then Pete scooped out the remaining dirt. With everyone helping, they lifted the pole and set it in place. Pete shoveled loose soil around the base and the children stamped it down firmly with their feet.

Old Ben chuckled. "Now we're back in business. I feel more at home with my totem looking out on the street."

"In Alaska do the totem poles face the street?" Ricky asked.

Mr. Roebuck replied that the Indians' totems faced their own particular highways, which were the rivers and the ocean. "That was so other Indians, while passing, could see the great carved figures," he explained.

Pam spoke up. "Old Ben, will you tell us more about the totem-pole riddle?"

The old sourdough said the mysterious missing pole was a raven totem. It had disappeared from a Haida Indian village.

"Did somebody take it?" Holly asked.

Old Ben nodded. "The totem was stolen because it contained a great secret."

"Hidden in the pole?" Pete wanted to know.

"That's right," the Alaskan said. "On this particular totem there was a hole in the back of the raven's head." Such holes, he explained, were made to contain the ashes of the dead chief. "Well, in this hole," he went on, "or perhaps somewhere else on the totem, a great secret was supposed to be hidden. The Indians said it would bring good fortune to the finder."

"Please tell us more," Pam begged.

But before he had a chance to do this, Mrs. Hollister drove up in the family station wagon. She was introduced to the old man and admired his work. Then, turning to her children, she said:

"We must hurry home."

"Something the matter?" Pete asked.

"There's a great surprise awaiting you at the house," their mother declared.

CHAPTER 5

WONDERFUL NEWS

As Mrs. Hollister drove up to their house, the children saw a new automobile standing at the curb.

"Is that a clue to the surprise?" Ricky asked.

His mother nodded. "See what's in the living room."

The children piled out of the station wagon and ran into the house.

"Uncle Russ!" Pete cried out.

"Aunt Marge!" Pam shrieked and ran over to hug a pretty, dark-haired woman.

"And Teddy and Jean!" said Ricky.

The Hollisters were always overjoyed to see these relatives. Uncle Russ looked very much like Mr. Hollister, who was his older brother. The visitors lived in Crestwood, the town where the Shoreham Hollisters used to reside.

Teddy and Jean instantly began to talk excitedly with their cousins. Jean was nine years old and a special pal of Pam's. She had straight chestnut-colored hair and dimples. Jean owned a pony and a pair of cocker spaniels.

Her brother Teddy was eleven. He had black hair

and gray eyes. Teddy was just as lively as Pete and looked somewhat like him, although he was an inch shorter.

The Shoreham Hollisters were especially proud of Uncle Russ. He was a cartoonist and drew a comic strip for many newspapers all over the country.

Sue tugged her uncle by the hand. "Come on, Uncle Russ," she begged. "We have to do our upside-down trick, you know."

This happened every time the handsome cartoonist visited his nieces and nephews. The tall man reached down, grabbed the little girl and set her on his shoulders.

Sue's eyes widened with delight. "Here we go!" she cried.

Her uncle bent his head forward and somersaulted Sue to the floor. After repeating the trick several times he put Sue down, straightened his necktie and smoothed out his mussed-up hair.

In a little while Mr. Hollister returned from *The Trading Post*. After a rugged handshake with his brother, he said, "Are you on a vacation, Russ?"

"Yes. We're returning from a stay at the shore," he replied. Then Uncle Russ frowned slightly. "John, I have a problem."

"Crickets, Uncle Russ!" Pete interjected. "Is there any way we can help you?"

The cartoonist smiled. "Perhaps you can."

He told them that he had temporarily run out of ideas for his comic strip. "I can't figure out where to take my characters on their next adventure. I thought a vacation with my family would give me some new thoughts, but——"

Pam's eyes shone brightly with excitement. "Oh, I know what, Uncle Russ!" she declared. "Why not make a comic strip about Alaska!"

"Alaska? What made you think of that?"

Instantly all the Hollister children started to chatter at the same time. Uncle Russ could make out words like "totem pole," "Old Ben," and "mysterious wilderness."

"Hold on," he said, holding up his hands and laughing. "What enthusiasm!"

Pam, as spokesman for the group, told the story of Old Ben and the totem pole. "And besides," she said, "there's a mystery about a raven totem. Could you make a comic strip on that, Uncle Russ?"

"It's a good idea," he replied. "What do you think of it, John?"

"First rate," the children's father said. "I recall that the country is wild and dangerous and has deep fiords."

Uncle Russ held his hand to his chin and thought earnestly. "Give me time to mull it over," he said. "Maybe Alaska *will* be the background for my next strip."

"And now," Aunt Marge spoke up, "I'll give you something we brought."

"Candy!" Sue declared, jumping off her uncle's knee and dancing up and down.

"Lollipops!" Holly added.

Aunt Marge had a reputation of being an excellent candy cook. She made lollipops in all sizes and shapes.

Aunt Marge beckoned to Teddy and whispered to him, "In my suitcase."

Teddy raced upstairs where the visitors' luggage had been put. He returned a moment later with two packages and handed them to his mother. As her nieces and nephews crowded around, she opened one.

"Oh, what beautiful lollipops!" Pam exclaimed.

"These creatures are all from the sea," said Aunt Marge.

She gave Sue a green walrus and Holly a brown seal. Pam received a pink salmon lollipop.

"I have two whales for the boys," Aunt Marge declared. "Who wants the black licorice one?"

Pete and Ricky looked at each other. Neither wanted to be greedy.

Pete grinned at his younger brother. "You take the licorice one, Ricky. I know you like it best."

"Thanks, Pete."

Aunt Marge gave Pete a white-whale candy. "I call it Moby Dick," she said.

In the boxes there was also an assortment of hard candies which Aunt Marge offered to Mr. and Mrs. Hollister.

Just then Sue put the walrus's head in her mouth. *Crunch!*

"Oh, I've broken a tooth!" Sue cried out.

44

Mrs. Hollister said worriedly, "Open your mouth and let me see."

Hearing the anxiety in her mother's voice, the little girl beamed. "Oh, not my tooth, Mommy. The walrus's tooth."

"That's a tusk, silly," Ricky said as his little sister munched on the bit of candy.

At Aunt Marge's suggestion the children put their candy aside until after lunch, which was served immediately by Mrs. Hollister. "Eat the lollipops for dessert," she said.

When Uncle Russ finished his meal, he said, "I'm going to phone my office long distance."

"About Alaska?" Ricky asked.

Uncle Russ grinned boyishly and nodded as he went off. A few minutes later he reported:

"They'll call me back and let me know."

The seven cousins played tag during the afternoon and then went for a swim off the dock. The water of Pine Lake was still rather chilly so they did not stay in long. Besides they heard the telephone ringing and eagerly ran back to the house in case it might be for Uncle Russ. It was.

In a moment the cartoonist came onto the front porch where the children had gathered.

"Great news for everyone!" he said.

"Are you going to Alaska, Uncle Russ, and make cartoons about totem poles?"

"Better than that. How would you all like to come with me?"

"Crickets!" Pete shouted. "You mean it?"

Uncle Russ excitedly said his company owned a large airplane which carried many passengers and had two pilots.

"I may have the use of it to fly to Alaska and back," their uncle said, adding that the plane could carry them all if they would like to go.

"Yikes!" Ricky exclaimed. He dashed off the porch and did a cartwheel on the lawn. "We're going to totem-pole land! Hurray! Hurray!"

When Mr. Hollister returned from *The Trading Post* that evening he was the most surprised man in Shoreham. "You mean you'll all fly to Alaska?"

"Sure," his brother said. "And you come along too, John."

Mr. Hollister said he wished he might, but his busy season was starting and he could not leave *The Trading Post*. When his wife mentioned that he should not be left alone, the store owner laughed.

"I'll manage all right," he said. "You all go." He winked at Sue. "Zip will take care of me and White Nose and the kittens, too!"

Plans were made for the company airplane to land at the Shoreham airport in two days. This would give everyone a chance to pack for the trip.

"And what say we have a picnic after church tomorrow to celebrate?" Mr. Hollister suggested.

"That would be great," Pete exclaimed.

"May we invite our friends, Mother?" Pam asked.

"Yes dear. Tell them two o'clock."

By the time telephone invitations had been extended and picnic food purchased, evening had come and the children retired to their rooms thinking about the fun they would have on the trip.

Sunday morning dawned clear and cool. The two families attended church. Later, the cousins gathered in the back yard. There was a long, whispered conversation. Then, giggling among themselves, the children trooped upstairs to the spacious attic on the third floor.

"The things should be right over here in this box," Pam told the others. "We put them back after Halloween."

"I want to wear the old witch one," Holly declared.

"Sssh!" Pam said. "The grownups might hear us. This is going to be a surprise."

Pam opened the lid of the box and Pete said, "You were right, Sis. Let's try them on now."

As the children busied themselves with their secret in the attic, Uncle Russ helped Mr. Hollister carry a portable grill from the garage to the back yard bordering Pine Lake. He set it beside a barberry hedge.

"Pete can get the charcoal and be the chef," Mr. Hollister said. Just then his son ran from the house, followed by Teddy. The boys were grinning broadly.

"What are you up to?" Uncle Russ asked.

The boys said nothing but went about preparing the fire. Then they brought hamburgers and frankfurters from the refrigerator and laid them on a shelf extending from the side of the barbecue grill.

About half past one the Hollisters' guests began to

They busied themselves with their secret.

arrive. Jeff and Ann Hunter were the first to race into the yard.

Jeff was eight. He had dark, straight hair and blue eyes and looked like his sister Ann. She was ten, and had curly hair which hung in ringlets. Her long black lashes made her gray eyes look large and pretty.

"Hi, everybody!" said Ann, and Jeff added, looking toward the grill, "Um. Good. And I'm hungry!"

No introductions were necessary because the Hollister cousins had visited in Shoreham before.

Donna Martin skipped in next and at once started looking for the kittens. Then Dave Mead hurried in. He immediately went to help Pete light the charcoal.

After it had become cherry red, the boys carried a long table and picnic benches from the Hollisters' big garage and set them up on the lawn. The girls spread the table with a snowy white cloth and set places with paper plates and cups.

Mrs. Hollister called from the house, "Time to put the meat on the fire, boys."

Pete reached for the hamburger patties and frankfurters. As he did, Dave glanced up. What he saw caused him to cry out in dismay!

Into the picnic spot bounded four mongrel dogs. Sniffing the aroma of the meat which Pete had laid on the grill, they yelped and barked and jumped up toward the shelf.

"Scat! Get out!" Pete cried as a black dog leaped up and tried to grab a string of frankfurters.

Pam shrieked. "They'll ruin our picnic!"

CHAPTER 6

HOLLY PLAYS AIR HOSTESS

ZIP, hearing the barking of the mongrels, raced from under a willow tree near the shore. He nipped at the legs of one of the dogs and chased him out of the yard. But the other three animals persisted in pawing about the food.

As everyone tried to chase them away, Ricky ran for the garden hose, which lay connected at the side of the house. Calling to Holly to turn on the water, he dragged the hose toward the dogs.

Swish! A stream of cold water sprayed over the intruders. Putting their tails between their legs, the dogs ran off.

As the commotion ceased, Pam thought she heard snickering behind the barberry hedge. Tiptoeing over, she caught sight of Joey and Will crouching low. Their arms were covered with a brown stain which she recognized instantly as poison-ivy medicine.

"We nearly ruined their picnic," Will whispered.

"Yes," Joey replied, unaware that Pam had spied them. "Sicking those mutts on the party was a great idea."

"But you were fooled!" Pam called out clearly.

51

Startled, the bullies dashed off, shamefaced at being discovered.

Mrs. Hollister gave a great sigh. "Maybe those boys will turn over a new leaf some day."

Holly pursed her lips and said, "Mother, I think they've used up a book already."

"What do you mean?"

"They've already turned lots of pages, but it doesn't seem to do any good."

Everyone chuckled. Pete gave Zip a juicy raw hamburger for his efforts and the dog gobbled it instantly.

Soon the aroma of sizzling hamburgers and frankfurters filled the air. When the meat was cooked, Pete tossed the burgers and franks onto a platter which Pam carried to the picnic table.

What a jolly time everyone had! The meat, potato salad, pickles, olives, hot rolls, and tomatoes were delicious, and the bright conversation added to the enjoyment of the picnic. Mrs. Hollister surprised everyone with ice cream and strawberries for dessert.

When the meal was over, Jean stood up and announced, "Now for another surprise!"

"What is it?" the Hunter children asked.

"Wait and see."

Pam, Ricky, Holly, and Teddy excused themselves and ran into the house. A few moments later they reappeared. But how different they looked! All wore grotesque masks.

Teddy had on a frog face. He sat down near the barberry hedge. Pam, who wore an owl false face, stood behind him. Next Holly, a horrible-looking witch, climbed up onto her sister's shoulders. Pam wobbled a bit under the weight but soon regained her balance. Then Dave and Pete hoisted Ricky, wearing a monkey mask, to the top of Holly's shoulders.

"Oh, dear!" Mrs. Hollister said worriedly. "Watch out, children!"

"Now I get it!" exclaimed Uncle Russ, who was seated on the end of a bench near the players. "This is a totem pole."

Unfortunately the players had not reckoned with Ricky's weight. He was too heavy for Holly's shoulders. Pam also began to stagger under the burden. Suddenly Ricky lost his balance. He fell over backward, heading straight for the prickly barberry hedge!

"Oh!" Sue screamed. "He'll get jaggers in him."

But Uncle Russ had leaped up. With one bound he caught Ricky in his arms.

"Crickets!" Pete declared. "How about that scene for your comic strip, Uncle Russ?"

"Not bad," the cartoonist said, laughing. "I've never seen faster action."

Everyone agreed it was a neat trick, and all were happy that Ricky was not full of scratches from the hedge. When the picnic was over, all agreed that it had been the jolliest one they had ever held.

That evening Pete and Pam took Uncle Russ to call on Mr. Roebuck. After looking at the totem, they went to the front door. Old Ben answered their ring and the children introduced their uncle.

"Come in, please," the sourdough said cordially and led them into his living room.

He was intrigued to hear that the Hollisters were going to Alaska and said, "I'll give you a letter of introduction to my friend Mr. Emmet Gallagher. He's living at the Alaska Pioneers' Home at Sitka, a residence for early settlers. He may have more information about the missing totem than I do. I'll ask him to tell you about it."

Excusing himself Old Ben went to a desk and wrote a letter. He put the message inside an envelope and handed it to Pam.

"Where would you say we should look for adventures?" Uncle Russ asked the old sourdough.

"You'll find plenty of excitement around Juneau and Sitka. I know you'll love Alaska," he said. "I wish I were going along to introduce you to some of my old friends."

When Pete and Pam returned home, they found the others packing for the trip. Next morning Mr. Hollister and Tinker, an elderly man who worked at *The Trading Post*, drove the cars to the Shoreham Airport. At ten o'clock a large silver plane from Uncle Russ's company landed on the airstrip.

"What a beauty!" exclaimed Ricky.

After the plane had taxied up and the motors had stopped, the pilot and copilot stepped out.

"Hi, Chet! Hello, Bud!" Uncle Russ said.

Chet, the pilot, was a short, stocky man. Bud, his copilot, was tall and lanky.

After introductions had been made, Chet said that he was thrilled to make a trip to Juneau again. "I used to fly there for an airline," he said.

After baggage had been stowed in the rear compartment, everyone said good-by to Mr. Hollister and Tinker. They then climbed in and took their seats.

"How roomy it is in the cabin!" Mrs. Hollister remarked.

"We could take twenty more passengers." Uncle Russ chuckled.

The children looked out the windows and waved to their father and Tinker. The plane taxied onto the runway, the motors roared, and soon the craft was air-borne.

Presently Chet's voice came over the loudspeaker. "We don't have a stewardess aboard to serve lunch," he said, "but if one of you girls would like to play the part, you will find a uniform hanging in the closet next to the galley."

Holly was eager to put it on immediately, but Mrs. Hollister reminded her that lunch time was two hours off.

As the plane roared through the air, the cousins amused themselves by looking at the interesting scenery below. But at twelve o'clock Sue said, "Mommy, I'm hungry."

Mrs. Hollister smiled. "Who would like to be the cook?"

"Please let me," Pam begged.

"And I'll be your assistant," Jean spoke up.

"May I be the stewardess, please, and serve people?" Holly asked. Mrs. Hollister nodded.

The galley was located in the middle of the airplane and had been provisioned by Chet and Bud before the start of the trip. Pam helped Holly put on the uniform from the tiny closet.

The little girl came strutting down the aisle. "At your service, passengers," she said brightly.

Everyone rocked with laughter. The blue skirt hung to the ground. The hostess's jacket was so long that the sleeves hid Holly's hands. Only the cap fit properly. The little girl wore it at a jaunty angle down over her right eye.

Pam and Jean efficiently went about preparing the food. Packages containing the entire meal had only to be heated. This the girls accomplished in a small warming oven.

When the food was ready, Ricky, Teddy, and Pete helped Holly serve it. "But I want to take Uncle Russ's myself," she insisted. "Jean, does your daddy like coffee?"

"Yes."

"With sugar?"

"Yes. Two spoonsful."

Holly reached for a tiny carton and poured the white crystals into the paper coffee cup. Balancing the tray carefully she took the lunch to her Uncle Russ.

He smiled as he took it. "Umm, I love good coffee."

He picked up the cup and took a sip. Then to every-

"At your service, passengers!"

one's amazement Uncle Russ made the funniest face the children had ever seen.

"Oh dear, what's the matter?" Holly cried out.

Her uncle could not talk. He began to cough and his eyes squinted. His mouth moved from one side to the other and he tried hard to gulp.

"It's—it's not too hot, is it?" Holly asked anxiously.

Finally Uncle Russ managed to say, "Who put salt in this?"

Holly spoke up in a small voice, her mouth down at the corners. "I—I guess I did. I thought it was sugar."

"Ugh!" her uncle said, as everyone started to chuckle.

"I'm terribly sorry," Holly apologized.

Pam got her uncle another cup of coffee, this time putting in real sugar.

During the afternoon the children helped to while away the time by walking forward and talking with the pilots. Then, after dinner, darkness fell and the Hollisters tilted back their chairs and went to sleep.

When the sleepy-eyed travelers wakened, dawn was streaking the eastern sky with rosy pink. Pam looked down and saw the green tracery of many small islands floating below them.

She hurried to assist her mother and aunt with the breakfast. Then the pilot's voice sounded over the intercom.

"We're flying over islands off the west coast of

Canada," he told them. "Our next stop will be Annette Island Airport in Alaska."

Several hours later, after they had finished lunch, Chet brought the plane lower and lower over the tree-studded rocky islands stretching below.

"We're coming into Annette now," the pilot announced. "Please fasten your seat belts."

As the plane landed, a feeling of excitement made Ricky's heart pound. "Yikes!" he exclaimed. "We're really in the land of the brown bears!"

Off to the west a snow-topped peak could be seen through misty clouds. Chet turned the plane about and taxied back toward a group of buildings on the west side of the runway.

The copilot's voice came on. "This is a chance to get out and stretch your legs, if you like, but please stay close to the plane."

The pilots let the stairs down from the exit door and everybody alighted. Exhilarated by the sweet, cool, fresh air, the children ran toward the tail of the plane while Chet and Bud supervised the refueling.

Sue pointed to the beautiful mountain and said, "I want to see it closer." She ran off.

"Come back here!" Holly cried out.

But the stiff wind, blowing past the little girl's ears, prevented her from hearing. Sue was now out on the airstrip.

Like a leaping deer Pete dashed after her, his heart pounding wildly. A big plane was settling down onto the runway!

CHAPTER 7

THE MISSING PURSES

IN A flash of speed Pete lunged forward. He grabbed Sue by the hand and pulled her from the path of the landing airplane just in time. He led her back to the others, who were quivering from the shock.

"Pete, you were brave to do that," his mother praised him. "And Sue dear, don't ever run off like that again!"

"I'm sorry, Mommy!"

Chet and Uncle Russ, whose conversation had been interrupted by the excitement, walked up to Mrs. Hollister and Aunt Marge. The cartoonist wore a frown as the pilot announced, "I have bad news for you. One of our motors hasn't been functioning properly. We'll have to lay over a few hours for repairs."

The children did not seem to mind the delay. "We can play games!" Holly chirped. "I brought some in my suitcase."

The pilot smiled. "I've heard you called the Happy Hollisters," he said. "Now I know why." He beckoned to the cousins. "This way to the waiting room."

The very fact that they were in Alaska seemed to be thrill enough for the cousins. After looking around the airport, they spent the afternoon with crayons, coloring books, checkers, and word games. The time passed quickly for them. It was not until after supper that Chet called out:

"We're ready now. All aboard!"

After taxiing onto the runway the large craft took off again. It flew high for a long time, then descended over a strip of water. Bud came back to point out the sights.

Mountains rose straight up on either side. Suddenly Pam pointed to the right and cried out, "Look down there! A city!"

"That's Juneau, capital of Alaska," Bud explained. "We're flying over Gastineau Channel."

Far below, a little city clung to the slope at the base of a towering mountain. Pam thought Juneau would slide into the channel were it not for the sturdy wharfs which rimmed the waterfront. One dock stood out above the others, because several yellow-winged seaplanes nosed against it. At that moment an amphibian was taking off across the water. Pam craned to watch its flight and in doing so spied a long gray structure halfway up the hillside.

"What's that?" she asked Bud.

"The Juneau gold mine. The city got its start when two miners named Juneau and Harris struck gold here many years ago."

Bud advised the passengers to fasten their seat belts and in a few minutes the plane made a graceful landing on a long airstrip. It came to a stop in front of a low brick building.

"Here we are," Chet announced. "Bud and I will fly back for you when you're ready to leave."

After thanking the fliers for the fine, safe trip, the Hollisters helped to unload their baggage. A large limousine took them into Juneau. It was a small city with narrow, winding streets and low buildings.

"This is kind of a tilted town," Holly remarked as they drove uphill to their hotel.

A suite on the third floor awaited them. Mrs. Hollister and her children had three adjoining rooms, while Uncle Russ's family occupied a pair across the small hall.

Pam glanced at her wrist watch. It was 10 P.M., yet it was still light outdoors!

"Time for bed," Mrs. Hollister said, smiling, "even in a land where the sun sometimes shines at midnight during the summer."

"And," said Uncle Russ, "in the winter it's sometimes dark here most of the day."

"I can't go to sleep in the daylight," Ricky protested.

Uncle Russ smiled. "Perhaps a stroll will make you all sleepy."

The family rode down in the elevator, trooped out of the hotel and along the narrow, concrete sidewalks. Presently Pete, who was in the lead, came to an extensive dock which ran parallel to the channel. Several people were ambling along the waterfront.

"Crickets!" Pete cried as the others caught up with him. "There's the seaplane basin we saw from the sky. Boy, it's neat!"

Jutting out into Gastineau Channel at right angles to the wharf was a floating dock. Resting lightly in the water beside it were two blue and yellow amphibian planes. On the dock itself three other seaplanes were parked before a hangar, where two mechanics worked over a motor.

"This is great!" Ricky cried out.

"And a lovely sight across the channel," Pam remarked. "Is that an island over there, Uncle Russ?"

The cartoonist did not know, but a bystander who overheard the question said the spot was Douglas Island. It was connected with the mainland by a long bridge.

As the little group started to walk on, Pam's mother asked the girl to hold her handbag. "My shoe is untied," Mrs. Hollister said.

Pam, who carried a small purse of her own, slipped it inside the larger bag, then ran ahead to catch up to the others. Her mother, hurrying after them a moment later, asked suddenly, "Where are Ricky and Holly?"

Pete whirled around. "Crickets! They were here a few seconds ago." He shouted for them, but there was no answer.

"Don't worry, Mother, we'll find them," Pam said consolingly.

She laid the handbag on a ledge beside which her mother was standing, then joined Pete, Teddy, and

Jean. They ran to the southerly end of the dock. The missing children were not there.

"They must have gone the other way," Pete declared, starting back. Suddenly he burst out, "There! I think I see them!"

"Where?"

"Over by the planes."

Pete and Pam dashed along the wooden planking, turned the corner of the dock, and hurried to the spot where the two men were working.

"You can't come through here," one of them said sternly.

"We're looking for our lost brother and sister," Pete explained.

"We didn't see anybody," the other fellow remarked.

Pam pointed to one of the aircraft lying in the water. It bobbed slightly from one side to the other.

"Hey, somebody's in there!" the first mechanic said.

"We'll see," Pete offered. He and Pam jumped down two feet onto the floating dock and ran over to the plane. The door was half open. Pete looked in. "Come out of there!" he exclaimed. "Everyone's looking for you."

Ricky and Holly stepped out, surprised expressions on their faces.

"We were only examining the plane," Ricky said. "It's keen!"

By this time the two mechanics were at their side.

65

"Outsiders aren't allowed on the dock," Pete told them.

They returned to the rest of the group and Ricky and Holly apologized for frightening everyone. Then the group headed for the hotel.

Mrs. Hollister glanced at Pam. "Where's my bag, dear?"

Pam stood still and a worried expression came over her face. "I laid it on the dock when I ran after Ricky and Holly. I—I thought you'd pick it up."

When Mrs. Hollister said she had not, everyone hastened back to the spot.

The bag was gone!

"Oh dear!" Mrs. Hollister exclaimed. "I had a good bit of money in it!"

Pam was on the verge of tears. "And my purse was inside it with Mr. Roebuck's letter and my beautiful silver pencil." She had received the sterling silver gift on her previous birthday. Designed with attractive scrollwork, it was one of her prized possessions. Pam could keep the tears back no longer. She put her arms around Mrs. Hollister and wept.

"There now," said Uncle Russ soothingly. "Don't take it so hard. I'm sure we'll find the bags."

But a search of the dock in the waning light gave no clue to the lost purses. Passers-by were questioned to no avail.

"Do you suppose the purses were stolen?" Ricky asked.

"Maybe they fell into the water," Pete said.

"Or perhaps somebody picked them up and took them to the police," Jean suggested hopefully.

Pete volunteered to telephone headquarters and ran to a booth in a nearby store. He emerged a few minutes later with a sad look. No purses had been reported as found. The city's patrolmen, however, would be ordered to look for the lost articles.

By now it had grown too dark for further search. Mrs. Hollister thought they should return to the hotel. Disappointed, they left the dock. Back in their rooms, the Hollisters went to bed at once and soon fell asleep.

Sue was the first to awaken. She crept out of her bed and went to the window. The sun was up again. The little girl pranced around the room crying loudly, "Wake up, Mommy! It's time to look for your bag."

Mrs. Hollister opened her eyes sleepily. "My, but I'm tired," she said, as she sat on the edge of the bed and stretched her arms. Then she glanced at her watch.

"Why Sue, you little monkey! It's only three o'clock in the morning!"

"But look, it's light outside. And the birdies are singing," Sue pointed out. "Maybe your watch has stopped, Mommy."

Mrs. Hollister telephoned the desk clerk. It was true —only three o'clock.

"Now back to bed," Mrs. Hollister said as she kissed her daughter. This time she pulled the shades down all the way.

When Mrs. Hollister awakened again, it was 8 A.M. She aroused her children.

From the sounds in the rooms across the little hallway, they were sure that Uncle Russ, Aunt Marge, Teddy, and Jean also were getting ready for breakfast. In a short time they all met in the hall.

"I want to play detective after breakfast," Ricky announced, "and hunt for clues to Mother's and Pam's bags."

"And I'll help," said Holly. "Where do we start?"

"We'll ask the men on the seaplane dock."

Everyone decided to go and set off at nine-thirty. The first person they saw was a stocky young pilot with a captain's bars on his sleeves. Uncle Russ introduced himself and learned that the flier's name was Lund.

"We're looking for a handbag containing a purse which was lost here on the dock last night," the cartoonist told him. "Did you hear of anyone finding such a bag?"

Captain Lund said no, then added, "Wait! I remember seeing a man pick up something."

"Was it a dark color?" Pam asked hopefully.

"Yes, it was," the pilot replied. "I saw the fellow put the article under his shirt."

"Where did the man go?" Holly asked.

Captain Lund said he had walked into the waiting room of the airlines' ticket office. The words were barely out of the pilot's mouth, when Pete and Teddy dashed into the building. The other children joined them and they searched frantically.

Pam was the first to spy Mrs. Hollister's handbag. "Here it is!" she screamed excitedly.

The handbag, which was lying under a long bench, was open. Pam picked it up, glanced inside and said bitterly:

"Oh, Mother, everything's gone! Even my purse!"

Uncle Russ examined the bag carefully. Indeed, it had been ransacked. "This is certainly tough luck," he said.

"And the important letter for Mr. Gallagher!" Pam wailed. "What'll we do now?"

Pete tried to comfort his sister by saying he was sure they could explain their case to the old sourdough at the Pioneers' Home.

"Yes," Mrs. Hollister agreed. "I'm sure he'll understand."

The Hollisters walked glumly from the waiting room. Their first day in Alaska was starting out far from happily.

Seeing their long faces, Uncle Russ said cheerfully, "Come now. I'm sure everything will turn out all right. What would you all like to do?"

"Visit a museum," Jean suggested. "Maybe we can find a clue to the missing totem pole Old Ben told you about."

"Yes," Holly chimed in. "Let's find the secret of the wooden faces!"

Pete asked a boy who was passing by where they could find the museum.

"Take this street," the lad said, smiling. "It leads up the hill to a large stone building. The museum is in there."

"Thank you." Pete led the way and a few minutes later the visitors entered the museum.

They were met by the curator, who stepped out of his glass-enclosed office to greet them. He was a smiling man of medium height who wore a gray sports jacket and shell-rimmed glasses. The children liked him instantly.

After listening to their story, the curator, whose name was Mr. Kay, said he had never heard of the missing pole, but added, "You're welcome to look around. We have a few totem poles. And there are many Eskimo and Indian relics to interest the children."

The museum was filled with native weapons, utensils, works of art, and even a large stuffed brown bear. Ricky and Teddy were especially interested in a kayak made of skin, while Pete and Pam examined several ancient totems.

Uncle Russ, meanwhile, sketched a collection of Haida Indian dolls as the others looked on admiringly. Suddenly Pam nudged him and pointed to a man standing at the back of the museum. The fellow was examining an old weather-beaten totem pole. He thrust his hand into a hole at the back of the relic.

70

"Oh, Mother, everything's gone!"

Then he took a knife from his pocket and began to scratch the half-rotted wood.

"He shouldn't do that, should he?" Pam whispered.

"No," Uncle Russ agreed.

Because Mr. Kay was busy in his office, the cartoonist put down his sketching pad and approached the man. "You can't deface things in a museum," he warned the fellow.

The man glared at Russell Hollister. He was short, thin, and one shoulder was hiked higher than the other.

"Mind your business," the shifty-eyed man said. He reached into his pocket and pulled out a pencil and a piece of paper. As he wrote something hastily on it, Pam gasped.

"My silver pencil!" she cried out.

CHAPTER 8

A MILLION ICE CUBES

WHEN Pam cried out, the rough-looking man jammed the silver pencil and paper into his pocket, turned and fled from the museum. Pete, Ricky, and Teddy dashed after him, with Uncle Russ close on their heels.

But the suspect was wily. He did not run down the street. Instead, he slipped into a store across the way and raced out the rear door. Then, running down an alley, he disappeared from sight.

His pursuers finally came to a halt, looking disappointed. "We'll catch that man next time we see him!" Teddy vowed.

"And make him return Mother's money and Pam's pencil and Mr. Roebuck's note!" declared Pete.

"Nice try," Uncle Russ commented as they returned to the museum. He added, "I wonder if Mr. Kay recognized that man."

The curator said he had caught a glimpse of the fugitive. "He looked like Abalone Farley."

Mr. Kay explained that Abalone was an unscrupulous fisherman who operated in the Sitka-Juneau area. On several occasions he had been caught raiding halibut lines and had spent several months in prison.

"My goodness, he's a bad one," Mrs. Hollister exclaimed.

Mr. Kay nodded. He cautioned the Hollisters to be careful and suggested that they notify the police immediately.

Using the telephone in the curator's office, Uncle Russ called police headquarters. After hearing the report, the desk sergeant said his men would search the downtown area immediately for Farley, whose description they knew well.

"We'll call you back shortly," the officer said.

While awaiting a reply, the Hollisters chatted with Mr. Kay. The friendly man showed much interest not only in the Hollisters' mystery but also in Uncle Russ's comic strip. He said he had made a study of totem poles and would be happy to answer any questions they had.

"Can anyone read a totem pole?" Jean asked him. "Or just Indians?"

Mr. Kay replied that totem poles were not read but recognized. They contained nothing more nor less than memory devices. These hints would recall a story to a person, provided he already knew it.

In answer to a question from Pete, Mr. Kay said that most of the stories carved on totem poles were taken from legends of the clans.

"Principal among them are the exploits of Raven, a hero to the Indians in the northwest area."

"And I'll bet they're a million years old!" Holly declared.

"No, indeed not." Mr. Kay told the Hollisters that most totem poles, even though they looked ancient, had been carved in the nineteenth century. "Most of the ones you'll find in Alaska today are only a hundred years old or less."

When Ricky told the curator that Joey Brill had said totem poles were idols, Mr. Kay laughed. "That's nonsense, of course. They were used as house pillars; as places for burying the ashes of the dead; as memorials, as heraldic, potlatch, and ridicule poles."

Pam made a mental note of this information to use in school, then asked about the ridicule poles.

"That was to shame a person," Mr. Kay said. "Haida Indians sometimes carved a figure on a pole upside down for that purpose."

"What about the door-latch pole?" said Holly.

This made everyone laugh. "You mean the potlatch pole," the curator said with a chuckle. "Well, when an Indian chief became rich, he entertained his friends at a big feast. This was called the potlatch. At that time a totem pole would be erected to mark the event."

Before Mr. Kay had a chance to tell more about the interesting totems, the telephone rang. He answered it, then handed the instrument to Uncle Russ. Police headquarters was calling. After listening to the message, the cartoonist hung up.

"The police are hot on the trail!" he told the others. "They may catch that fellow Farley. He took off for

75

Sitka in an airplane and will be questioned when he arrives."

The police had learned that the pilot of the plane was their friend, Captain Lund. Contacted by radio, he had said that Farley was seated up front in the seat next to him. The suspect, who could not hear the conversation because of the engine's noise, would be searched upon landing at Sitka.

"Goody!" Holly exclaimed just as the telephone rang again.

Another message came in from headquarters, but this time the news was disappointing. The Hollisters were told that Farley had been searched after the plane had landed, but the pencil, Mrs. Hollister's money, and the letter had not been found on him.

Pam sighed. "Where did our good clues disappear?" she asked.

"Captain Lund thinks he knows," Uncle Russ added. He said that before landing, the flier had noticed Farley drop something out of the window next to him. It looked like a white handkerchief.

"Crickets!" Pete exclaimed. "I'll bet I know what happened. Farley made a handkerchief parachute and dropped everything he'd stolen into the water."

"But it would sink!" Teddy spoke up.

Pete suggested that Farley might have attached a piece of cork to the handkerchief. This would keep the package floating until he had a chance to retrieve it.

Pam was worried, however, that Farley might use

Old Ben's letter to Mr. Gallagher to get on the trail of the mysterious totem.

Jean suggested that they go to Sitka as quickly as possible and explain everything to Mr. Gallagher.

"But there are no more planes to Sitka today," Mr. Kay said. "You'll have to spend the night here."

Noticing how glum the children looked over the delay, the curator suggested that they visit Mendenhall Glacier during the evening. "It's only a few miles from here," he said, "and quite a sight."

They thanked him and went back to the hotel, where Uncle Russ telephoned to rent a station wagon. After supper the families drove out of town along a winding road and soon came to a breath-taking scene. Ahead of them was an ice-filled chasm between two mountain slopes.

"Yikes!" Ricky exclaimed. "A million ice cubes!"

The glacier sparkled blue-white in the distance, and as the travelers drew nearer they realized how vast it was.

"Whizzikers!" Teddy called out. "I've never seen so much ice in all my life!"

Coming to the end of the road, everyone got out and climbed over mounds of rock extending up to a frigid lake at the foot of the glacier.

"I feel mighty small," Pam said as she compared her size with the wall of ice stretching across the valley.

Uncle Russ's fingers fairly flew over his sketching

Jean reached for a little iceberg.

pad as he drew various views of the awesome panorama.

"Golly!" Teddy said. "How did all the ice get in here, Dad?"

His father explained that this resulted from an accumulation of snow high on the peaks farther inland. Moving slowly under great pressure, the snow changed to ice which moved at a snail's pace down the valley.

Pete noticed that the rocky wall on the right side of the glacier had been scarred deeply. He guessed it was from the movement of the ice.

"That's right," said his mother.

"And did it make these too?" Ricky asked, picking up a few white granite pebbles.

Mrs. Hollister said yes, the motion of the glacier had ground the stones to almost perfect roundness. The boys picked up handfuls and thrust them in their pockets.

"Souvenirs!" Teddy said with a grin.

By now the sun was hanging low over the mountain and the color of the ice changed from a pale hue to a rosy tint. Mrs. Hollister handed her camera to Pete, who took several pictures.

"I think we can get a better view from the other side of the lake," Pete said, and Uncle Russ agreed with his nephew.

They climbed inside the station wagon and drove back along the road. Uncle Russ turned right and finally came to the opposite shore of the chilly lake.

"Yikes! Look! Icebergs!" Ricky yelled as he jumped out of the car and ran toward the beach.

Chunks of ice, which had broken off the glacier, floated toward the shore. They were crystal clear.

Ricky picked up a small piece which had come aground on the pebbly beach. "Here's where I get a drink of ice-cold glacier." He grinned and began to suck on the piece. It tasted cold and delicious.

"I want a piece too," Jean said. Picking up a small stick on the shore, she reached far out to retrieve another berg that was floating away.

"There—I—can—get——" *Splash!* Jean fell into the icy water. Quickly struggling to the shore, she said, "Oh, I'm fr-freezing!"

Her mother and father helped to wring the water from her clothes. Then everyone hurried back to the car so she could return to Juneau quickly.

When they reached the hotel, Jean hurried to the elevator and went upstairs to change her clothes.

As her father stepped past the hotel desk, a policeman suddenly confronted him. "I'm Officer John," he said. "Are you Mr. Hollister?" he asked.

"Yes, Officer."

"We have received a complaint against someone named Hollister," the policeman said gravely.

"Me?" Uncle Russ asked in shocked surprise.

"I'm not certain," the policeman continued. "Someone named Hollister took a wallet from an old man in Sitka this afternoon."

Until now, the children were too dumfounded to say a word.

Finally Pete found his voice. "What was the name of the man who was robbed?" he asked.

"Mr. Gallagher," Officer John replied.

CHAPTER 9

AN EXCITING RIDÉ

INSTANTLY the Hollister children wondered if the Mr. Gallagher who had been robbed was the one who lived in the Pioneers' Home at Sitka.

As Pete was about to ask Officer John this, Uncle Russ spoke up. "We haven't been to Sitka."

He explained where the Hollisters had been during the day, and the policeman said, "I see."

Pete now asked his question and Officer John said yes, the man who had been robbed lived at the Pioneers' Home.

"We had a letter of introduction to Mr. Gallagher," Pete went on, "and it was lost. We think Abalone Farley found it."

After Officer John had been convinced that an impostor had stolen the old pioneer's wallet, Pam asked, "Did Mr. Gallagher describe the thief?"

The policeman told her that unfortunately the old sourdough had poor eyesight and could not give a clear description of the fellow.

"We're going to Sitka tomorrow," Pete said. "Perhaps we can help find the rascal."

Officer John said he would be happy for any assistance the Hollisters might give him and wished them luck on their flight.

"Why is the bad man called Abalone?" Holly asked.

The policeman said that Farley had received the nickname many years before. He was fond of abalone, a shellfish found along the coast.

"It's something like an oyster," Officer John explained, "and is very tasty. Abalones have beautiful shells, too. You children may find some at Sitka."

Since the mistaken identity charge had been cleared up, the policeman said good-by to the Hollisters and left the hotel.

Next morning the baggage was packed again and the boys helped carry the suitcases to the airlines office. As Uncle Russ purchased tickets, the clerk smiled and said:

"Lucky you came early, Mr. Hollister. You can all go together in one plane." He smiled. "By the way, it won't hold any more."

Hearing this, Jean looked sad. "You mean no one else can fly to Sitka today?"

The airlines man smiled and said that an extra plane would take off shortly afterward with other passengers.

"It'll be just like having a private plane again," said Pam.

"I'll be the hostess," Holly suggested, giggling.

This time the children were allowed to walk onto the floating dock and look at the twin-motored amphibian plane which would take them to the old capital.

As an attendant stored the baggage in a rear compartment, Captain Lund approached the group. He was wearing a blue uniform and a peaked pilot's cap. "Are you going to pilot us?" Pete asked, smiling.

"Yes, I am. Say, any news about the handbag?"

Pete told him what little they knew. "We're going to find out more when we get to Sitka."

The boy now pointed to a long building which housed the gold mine on the side of the hill. "Could we go up there sometime and look around, Captain Lund?"

"Nobody's allowed in the old mine now," the flier replied.

Ricky had been staring at the place. "That would be a swell place for anybody to hide," he said.

The captain thought so, too. He said that the old shafts ran for miles into the hill and deep underground. "It's now considered too dangerous to be explored by visitors. Too bad. It's very interesting."

Now he looked at Uncle Russ, smiled, and asked, "All set for Sitka?"

"Yes."

"May I sit up front with you?" Pete requested.

"Sure thing."

The Hollisters stepped from the dock into the seaplane and Pete made his way forward to the bucket seat at the right side of Captain Lund's.

The pilot told Pete to close the sliding window beside him. "The wind will be pretty strong," he said.

Now he started the motors. Then, reaching overhead, the captain pushed a lever which made the motors go faster and the plane taxied into Gastineau Channel.

As the wind was coming from the north, Captain Lund guided his craft far out into the water, then turned into the stiff breeze.

"Here we go!" he said.

Pete's heart pounded with excitement. The noise increased in crescendo. Now the airplane was slapping the wave tops and rushing across the blue-green water.

Pete noticed that they were heading straight for the bridge connecting Juneau and Douglas Island and going at a furious pace. When would the plane soar skyward and miss it?

Thump! Thump! The bottom of the flying boat skimmed over the water. The bridge loomed closer.

Now the boy's heart raced wildly. He glanced at the pilot. How could they ever get into the air before reaching the steel span?

Captain Lund's face showed no sign of anxiety and Pete tried not to be frightened. Suddenly both motors roared with a fearful din.

The airplane whizzed under the bridge!

No sooner was it on the other side than *zoom*, the craft lifted sharply into the air. Pete breathed a sigh of relief as the plane gained altitude.

Captain Lund headed north and banked left around the tip of Douglas Island before continuing in a southwesterly direction.

Below, on the sparkling water, the green-clad islands passed beneath the fliers like giant rafts. Now Pete could see white-capped mountains looming in the distance.

He leaned toward the captain and shouted, "Do we go over those?"

The pilot nodded. About twenty minutes later the tallest of the peaks stood like a snow-capped sentinel ahead of them.

"What's that called?" the boy queried.

"Mount Annahootz. Named for a friendly Indian chief. It's nearly five thousand feet high."

As the plane crossed the mountain top, Captain Lund touched Pete's arm and pointed down. Far below, half a dozen brown dots were moving on the snow. The pilot reached to a pocket on his left and took out a pair of binoculars which he handed to Pete. The boy trained them on the objects below.

"Mountain goats!" he exclaimed.

The beautiful animals with their curved horns took giant leaps down the mountainside and disappeared behind a craggy rock formation. Pete grinned and handed the glasses back.

Once over the top of Annahootz, the plane nosed down into a deep glide toward Sitka. The city nestled on the shore of a snug harbor far beneath them. Captain Lund cut the motors. Now he and Pete could speak without shouting, and the pilot told the boy to look at the scene ahead. On an island directly across the channel from the small town rose another beautiful mountain.

"It looks like pictures of Fujiyama in Japan," Pete remarked.

"It's often called the Fujiyama of North America," the pilot said, "but its name is Mount Edgecumbe. And see those long white buildings? That's a hospital for Eskimos and Indians. They come here from all over Alaska."

The whistling of the wind on the seaplane's wings grew fainter as it glided low over the water. Pete remarked that he had never seen so many small islands in one place.

"There are scores of them in this harbor," the pilot said, as he banked the plane. Then, with a few little bounces, it settled into the water.

During the flight Pete had not heard a sound from the other Hollisters. Now the cousins' voices broke into excited shouts as the plane taxied up to a low wooden dock.

"I see a totem pole!" Holly exclaimed.

"Yikes! Look how tall it is!" Ricky added.

The passengers thanked Captain Lund for a fine trip and debarked. A porter from the hotel where Uncle Russ had arranged to stay carried the luggage off. Meanwhile, the children raced on ahead to the small park facing the water, where the totem pole stood. It was higher than any they had yet seen. The

"Those Indians look sad!"

Hollisters' faces broke into smiles as they looked up at the odd wooden faces grinning down.

Mrs. Hollister, Uncle Russ, and Aunt Marge also walked over to gaze at the towering totem. The cartoonist had his pad and pencil out in a flash. He was making a sketch when a boy and girl walked past. Both looked seriously at the ground, paying no attention to the visitors.

Pam saw at once that they were Indians. The lad was about fourteen. He had a round face, dark complexion, and large brown eyes. In his left hand he held a large silvery salmon by the gills. It was two feet long.

"Wow! What a whopper!" Ricky exclaimed admiringly, but the boy did not smile.

The Indian girl, who looked like the boy, was about Pam's age. Her black hair was cut in a bob and bangs.

"Gosh! They look sad," Teddy remarked.

The girl passed close enough to hear this remark and Pam noticed that tears rolled down her cheeks. On impulse Pam stepped up to her.

"Are you in trouble?" she asked kindly.

The Indian girl began to sob and Pam was embarrassed. But Mrs. Hollister hurried to her side and put an arm around the little girl's shoulders.

"What is the matter, dear?"

The child wept so hard that she could not reply, but the boy said, "My sister and I just came back from fishing. As we were going to tie up our boat, a man jumped in and went off in it."

"You mean he stole your boat?" Pete asked.

"Yes," the Indian boy said. "Now Beth and I won't be able to enter the Salmon Derby!"

CHAPTER 10

THE PIONEER'S STORY

AFTER Pam and her mother had calmed the Indian girl, the Alaskan children introduced themselves as Rossy and Beth Kindue. They said their stolen motorboat, which belonged to the family, was red, with the flag of Alaska painted on either side of the bow.

"Oh, I thought you had the American flag in Alaska," Pam said.

Hearing this, Beth wiped away her tears. "Yes," she said, "we do have the Stars and Stripes, but we have our own territorial flag as well."

Beth said the Alaskan flag was beautiful with the Big Dipper and North Star against a blue background.

"An Indian child designed it," she added proudly.

"Now tell us about the Salmon Derby," Pete said.

Sue pursed her mouth. "Is it sort of like a hat for a fish to wear?"

The others laughed and Rossy said, "It's a contest."

He explained that the Salmon Derby was a three-day fishing event which took place at Sitka each year. There were prizes given for those who caught the largest salmon.

"Can't you borrow another boat," Ricky asked, "and still get in the Salmon Derby?"

The Indians explained that the Derby was so popular that every boat in the area had been signed up for the event. The children's sad look returned.

"We'll help you find yours!" Pete declared with determination.

"Oh, thank you!" Beth replied.

Rossy grinned. "I'm going to tell Police Chief Harris about our boat as soon as I take this fish home. With everybody helping, perhaps we can find the thief."

Beth said her family lived in the Indian section of Sitka and pointed to a street to the left of the main avenue.

"We'll see you later," she said as they hurried off. The Hollisters waved good-by and walked toward their hotel, located on the main avenue not far from the waterfront. Across the street from it stood a large building made of tan brick. It sat on a grassy knoll, with sidewalks crisscrossing expansive green lawns.

In front of the building stood a bronze statue of an old Alaskan sourdough. He wore a battered felt hat and a large mustache. Slung over his back was a load of camping gear. In his left hand he carried a rifle and in his right a walking stick.

The statue looked down on several green benches occupied by elderly men chatting in the bright sunshine.

"The Alaska Pioneers' Home!" Pam exclaimed.

Sue nudged Jean as they walked up the street. "Are those the old-timers, do you suppose?" she asked.

"They must be."

"I wonder which one is Mr. Gallagher."

Overhearing the conversation, Mrs. Hollister said that they would look for Mr. Roebuck's sourdough friend after they had unpacked their luggage.

The Hollisters filled the small lobby of the hotel as they entered, and Uncle Russ signed them in. The manager was a husky man with sandy hair. He introduced himself as Mr. Carr and shook hands with Uncle Russ.

"Your rooms are on the second floor," Mr. Carr said. "You'll find your baggage up there already."

Ricky, Holly, and Sue hurried upstairs ahead of the others and were the first to finish unpacking.

"May we three go out and play?" Holly asked her mother. When Mrs. Hollister said yes, the children skipped downstairs.

Once in the lobby, they decided to go out to the street. Then they crossed to the other side, where a low stone wall banked the grassy lawn of the Pioneers' Home.

Ricky hoisted Sue to the top of the wall. Then he and Holly scrambled up and the three children sat down on the grass. Several old men, walking slowly along the sidewalk, smiled at the children.

"Let's have a game of 'gray goose,'" Holly suggested.

"We need more players," Ricky said.

"Oh, look! I see Beth and Rossy with another little girl," Holly remarked.

Ricky called them. The Indian children came over and Beth introduced them to her sister Sasha, who was five. Rossy said they were on their way to Chief Harris.

"Stay a little while and play with us," Holly begged.

"All right, but just for a few minutes," Rossy said.

The Kindue children had not heard of "gray goose." Holly explained that they all should sit on the grass in a circle. The one who was *it* would start the game by passing behind the children and tapping each one on the head and saying some color of goose, such as red goose, blue goose, green goose.

"When the one who's *it* says 'gray goose,'" Ricky continued, "the person who is tapped chases him around the circle and tries to tag him before he can return to the empty space."

Holly went on to explain that if the *it* person was caught, he must go to the center of the circle until someone was caught to replace him.

The Indians were delighted. "Who'll be *it*?" Beth chuckled.

Holly volunteered. The others sat in a circle, and the little girl skipped behind them, tapping each one on the head.

"Blue goose, pink goose, lavender goose," she called out as the Sitka youngsters giggled. Then she tapped Rossy on the head and shouted, "Gray goose!"

The Indian boy jumped up and chased Holly

"Oh, I'm sorry!"

around the circle. But she slipped into the empty spot before being tagged.

"Now you're *it*, Rossy!"

The Indian boy called out several colors before touching Ricky's head. "Gray goose!"

Ricky jumped up and chased Rossy. The Indian boy was a fast runner, so Ricky had to sprint extra hard. In doing so, he skidded on the grass and rolled over and over toward an elderly man with a cane limping along the sidewalk.

"Look out!" Holly cried.

Ricky, however, was spinning so fast that he fell off the stone edge and bumped into the man's legs. The old fellow teetered but managed to keep his balance.

"Oh, I'm sorry!" Ricky exclaimed, leaping to his feet.

The lame man walked gingerly toward a nearby bench and sat down. "I'm all right, little boy," he said.

The other children gathered around to make sure the old-timer was not hurt.

"We're all sorry," Holly said. "Will you please forgive us, Mr.———"

"Gallagher is my name."

Holly's mouth dropped open in surprise. "Mr. Gallagher!" she said. "Are you Ben Roebuck's friend?"

"Yes. How did you know that?" The sourdough bent forward to get a better look at the children.

"Well, please sit right where you are, Mr. Gallagher," the little girl begged. "I'm going to call my brother and sister and my mother and Uncle Russ."

Holly raced off. She returned in a few minutes with the rest of her family. When introductions were made, the Hollisters told their story.

Then Mr. Gallagher told how the impostor had robbed him. "He had a letter from Ben Roebuck, so I thought he was an honest man."

"Was the letter damp?" Pete asked quickly.

"Yes, it was. How could you guess that?"

Pete explained about Farley throwing the "parachute" handkerchief with the stolen articles out of the plane window. "I thought he'd go pick it up after he'd been searched."

Mr. Gallagher smiled. "You're a good detective, all right. I hope you find that scoundrel. To think I described the lost totem pole to him while he was picking my pocket! But I've had bad luck before. Many years ago somebody stole a fortune in gold nuggets from me."

"Oh dear!" Pam exclaimed. "That *is* bad luck!"

As Uncle Russ made a sketch of the old-timer, Aunt Marge asked him to tell them more about the mysterious totem.

The elderly man leaned back on the bench and tilted his hat forward to shield his eyes from the rays of the bright sun. Then he began.

"The totem Old Ben told you about with the treasure in it had a raven on the top holding a salmon in his claws. Beneath it was the killer whale, then a bear and a frog upside down.

"Goodness!" Holly interjected with a giggle. "The blood will rush to his make-believe head."

This made the others laugh and Pam remarked, "Maybe the frog was carved upside down because the Indians were making fun of it."

Mr. Gallagher said she was right. The frog represented the chief of the frog clan, who owed the leader of the killer whales ten sea otter furs. So the killer whale people carved the upside-down frog to ridicule their enemy. The sourdough added that the Haidas, who possessed the totem, had captured it from the killer whale clan.

"Why?" Pete asked.

"Because they said the killer whales had no right to use the raven on their totem." He smiled at the perplexed faces before him. "The old Indians had strange customs," he said.

The Hollisters also learned that the totem was said to have been hidden in the area of Sitka. "But just where I couldn't say," Mr. Gallagher concluded the story.

Pete was disturbed. "Now Abalone Farley has a head start in his search," the boy said. "He's probably the man who stole the Kindues' motorboat and is using it in his search. If he finds that treasure before we do——"

"Come on!" Beth urged, tugging Rossy by the

arm. "We must hurry and report our loss to the police chief."

While Mr. Gallagher had been talking, Sue and Sasha had wandered off. They were now engaged in a somersault race on the sloping lawn.

"Come back here!" Pam called as she ran toward them.

But the two little girls paid no attention. Head over heels they somersaulted closer and closer to the top of the stone wall!

CHAPTER 11

THE BLOCKHOUSE

ALL at once Pam saw a man in a blue uniform dash to the wall toward which Sue and Sasha were somersaulting.

As they tumbled over, he caught them both in his arms.

"That's Chief Harris!" Rossy cried out.

The chief stood on the sidewalk grinning at the two little girls. He was tall and portly and wore a small, bristly mustache.

"Ooh!" said Sue in surprise.

Then she and Sasha giggled as the officer placed them on the sidewalk.

"You two little cubs should watch where you're going," he said.

"Thank you for saving us," said Sue, rolling her eyes. Then she reached up and kissed him on the cheek.

The man's chuckles of amusement were quickly dispelled when Rossy told the chief about the theft of his boat.

"We think Abalone Farley did it," Pete spoke up,

"and is going to use it to look for a mysterious lost totem."

The officer took a pad from his pocket and made notes of what the children had told him. "We'll be on the lookout for Farley," he said. "But there are so many good hiding places in the bays and inlets that it will be hard to find him."

Hearing that all the Hollisters would join in the search, the chief smiled and said, "Good. All of you can be my deputies."

Chief Harris now told the visiting children that if they were interested in totems, Sitka had a park full of the old relics. "In fact," he added, "the place has been nicknamed Totem Park."

"Oh, we'd love to see them," Pam said. "How do we get there?"

"I'll show you," Rossy offered.

Beth said, "There's an old blockhouse in the park, too. It's only a mile from here."

It was decided that after supper that evening Beth and Rossy would act as guides and take all the Hollister children but Sue for a hike through the park.

"Its real name is Sitka National Monument," the chief said. Then he hurried off to look for Abalone Farley.

The Indian children returned home, where they had chores to do. But the Hollisters continued to walk around the town. They looked at shop windows until they came to a hardware-sporting goods store. Grinning, Pete beckoned the others to follow him inside.

He stopped and sniffed the air. "Um, this smells good as a trading post should!"

"It makes me a little homesick," Pam remarked.

When a clerk approached the children, Pete told him about their father's store in Shoreham.

"We'd like to take him a good-looking souvenir," the boy said.

"How about a fishing lure?" the clerk suggested. "A herring dodger is unique around here—they're made by the Indians."

The children looked at several of the highly polished copper spinners, and Pete finally bought one with a raven's head hammered into it.

At seven o'clock Beth and Rossy arrived at the hotel. The cousins joined them and they all trooped down the street together. Presently they passed an old Russian cathedral and came to a sparkling inlet.

"This is called Silver Bay," Rossy said. "It's very deep here."

Beth told the visitors that the Russians, who had once owned Alaska, built Sitka as their capital. Later, the United States bought the territory, and on October 18, 1867, the American flag was raised at Sitka for the first time.

"I'm glad Uncle Sam has it now," Rossy remarked.

Finally the hikers came to the entrance of Totem Park, which was flanked by two tall poles on either side of a wide path.

"This land is really a peninsula," Rossy said. "On

the left is the Indian River and on the right is Silver Bay."

As Ricky looked into the park, he remarked, "It's spooky in there."

The park was filled with Sitka spruce and western hemlock, which towered over a carpet of ferns, moss, devil's-club, and berry thickets. Large alder trees grew along the Indian River, a shallow stream which churned and gurgled over pebbly sand bars.

"You mean you don't want to go in?" Beth teased Ricky.

"Oh, sure."

As the children proceeded along the path, Jean said she had never seen a more beautiful place in her life.

"Yes, it's lovely now, but it was dangerous at one time," Beth said.

"What do you mean?" Pete asked.

"An ambush took place here on the shore of Silver Bay," Rossy replied.

He told his awed listeners that a party of Russians had landed here many years before. The Indians knew they were coming and set a trap for them.

"It was a fierce fight, and the Indians won."

"It's too bad they had to fight," Pam said with a sigh. But her cousin Teddy had a different thought. "Let's play Russians and Indians!" he cried out.

Ricky danced about and whooped wildly, eager for the game.

"Let's wait until we see the blockhouse," Pete suggested. "Where is it, Rossy?"

"Down the path a ways."

The forest was so thick that the sun was almost shut out. When the slanting rays did touch the totem poles, Pam thought they gave a weird appearance to the wooden faces.

"Beth," she asked, "are these totem poles ancient?"

The Indian girl said they had been carved by natives working for the government and were only replicas of originals made by her ancestors.

"Then I guess the treasure isn't in any of them," Pete ventured.

"I see the blockhouse!" Ricky shouted.

He and Teddy were the first in a race up to the large structure made of logs. It had a commanding view of Silver Bay.

"Let's choose sides," Jean said, "and play our game."

Ricky, Teddy, Jean, and Holly insisted upon banding together as "Indians" against the older children.

"All right," the others agreed, and Rossy said, "We 'Russians' will give you a head start. If we can capture you within twenty minutes, we'll bring you back to the blockhouse as our prisoners."

"If you don't, then you're our prisoners!" Ricky shouted.

Quickly the four younger children scampered through the woods and were soon out of sight.

"They're heading for Indian River," Beth said.

Her brother smiled. "We'll give them five minutes, then surround the whole bunch."

It was decided that Beth and Pete would move to the left, while Pam and Rossy would make a sweep to the right, finally meeting on the bank of the Indian River.

"But suppose they wade across it?" Pam asked.

"They won't," Rossy said with confidence.

"Why not?" Pete asked.

"Wait and you'll see."

Before they parted, Beth explained that many paths crossed Totem Park, so there was no danger of getting lost.

"Okay," Pete said. "Time's up. Let's get our prisoners!"

The four older children set off according to plan. Pam and Rossy passed a huge totem in a green clearing, and the girl stopped long enough to stare at the curious figure on top. It was a sorrowful-looking man wearing a tall stovepipe hat. A few minutes later they reached the shore of Indian River.

"It's so shallow, Rossy," Pam said, "they'll escape across it for sure."

Just then Pete and Beth trotted up. "Did you see anyone?"

"No."

Together the four searchers scanned the shore of the river. Two big trees, which had fallen from the bank, lay on the edge of the swirling current.

"I'll bet they're hiding down there," Pete guessed.

He ran forward with the others following. As he approached the huge trunk, four heads popped up.

"Ow! This is freezing!"

"We've caught you Indians!" Pete cried out. "You're our prisoners!"

"Ha-ha!" Ricky grinned. "Not yet!"

Pam saw that he and his three playmates held shoes and socks in their hands. Now they stepped quickly into the shallow water at the narrowest part of the stream and started across.

"Come on!" Pete commanded his group. "Let's get them!"

Rossy merely grinned. "They'll come back."

"Are you sure?" Pam asked.

Suddenly Teddy called out, "Ow! This is freezing!"

"Oooo!" Holly squealed. "I can't stand it any longer!"

Rossy chuckled. "That's the iciest water around here! It comes down from a snowy mountain peak."

Jean, too, shortly agreed to give up, saying that her feet were turning blue from the cold. As the four youngsters stepped out of the icy stream, they were captured.

Pam said, "Let's be kind to our poor Indian prisoners, Pete, and warm their feet before we start back."

"Okay. Sit down, you scamps."

As the four Hollister cousins rested on the log, the older children chafed their feet briskly until they were warm again. Once socks and shoes were donned, they all started back for the blockhouse.

"Oh, dear," said Jean, "how many years will I be a prisoner?"

"They're going to keep us in jail till the bears eat us," declared Ricky with a wink.

Just as the blockhouse came into view, however, Teddy made a dash for freedom. He raced toward the shore of Silver Bay, with Pete after him.

Suddenly Teddy stopped short. "Pete! Look at this!" he said, bending over to pick up something from the grass.

"Pam's silver pencil!" Pete exclaimed. His sister quickly identified it.

"Farley must be near here!" Pam said excitedly. "Maybe this is where he hid your boat, Rossy!"

Forgetting about their captives, the Hollisters and the Indian children ranged along the shore line looking for the stolen boat.

Coming onto a little cove, Pete noticed a motorboat lying ten yards off shore. The sun glinted off it in such a way that Pete could not make out the color instantly. He called to Rossy and the Indian boy ran to Pete's side.

"Is that your boat?" he asked.

Rossy squinted. Then he saw the flag of Alaska, with the Big Dipper and the North Star, painted on the bow.

"That's it, Pete!"

"Come on, let's get it!"

The boys quickly kicked off their shoes, peeled off their socks, and rolled up their trousers.

Their shouts of joy brought the other children, as the two boys started to wade into the water.

"Oh, I'm so happy," Beth said. "Now we can enter the Salmon Derby after all! I've always—oh!"

As Pete and Rossy splashed closer to the anchored boat, she had seen a man's head suddenly raise up over the gunwale. The others saw it, too.

On the shore Pam screamed, "It's Farley!"

The man glared at the children. "Get out of here!" he ordered.

He picked up an oar and swung it menacingly toward the two boys. Pete and Rossy paused a moment. With the speed of a trapped cat, Farley leaped up and started the motor.

"Come on!" Pete cried. "We can still get him!" He made a grab for the boat.

"Look out for the propeller!" Pam cried.

Pete obeyed the warning just in time. The motor roared and the stolen boat sped out into Silver Bay.

"Come back! Please give us our boat!" Beth pleaded tearfully, but Farley paid no attention.

Hunching low in the back seat, he guided the speeding craft across Silver Bay and disappeared among the shadows of the opposite shore.

"He won't get away next time!" Pete vowed as they all set off toward Sitka, but he noticed how discouraged the Indian children looked.

Back at the hotel Pete telephoned Chief Harris to tell him what had happened. "This will make it easier for us," the officer declared.

When the older Hollisters heard the story, they

were much concerned. "I do hope the police catch that thief soon," Aunt Marge said.

Uncle Russ made a series of sketches of the evening's adventure from the children's description. He grinned and said, "I'm really getting a fine comic strip out of your escapades."

Though it was still light outdoors, the hour was getting late. The younger children, weary, went to bed without argument. But Pete and Pam begged to stay up a little longer.

"The colors of the Alaskan sky at sunset are so beautiful," Pam said dreamily.

Pete added that he had never seen anything like it before. "The sun doesn't drop straight down," he said. "It drifts north on the horizon as if it hates to give up the day."

Pam chuckled. "Something like Sue fussing around when she doesn't want to go to bed."

Mrs. Hollister smiled, then gave the two children permission to stay up a little later. Pete and Pam went outside and joined Beth and Rossy, who had waited near the hotel.

"I know where we can get a splendid view of the harbor at sunset," Beth said. She led them down the street, then turned left up a flight of stone steps to a plot of high ground overlooking the water.

"It's wonderful," Pam said, breathing in the tangy sea air.

"This is where Alexander Baranof built his castle

when he ruled over Russian Sitka," Rossy told the visitors.

"What happened to it?" Pete asked, and Rossy said the castle had been destroyed many years before.

Suddenly the conversation ceased as the children heard the distant sound of a motorboat. Looking south, they peered hard at a craft speeding far out on Silver Bay.

"Our boat!" Rossy cried.

CHAPTER 12

THE INDIAN'S CLUE

EXCITED, the Hollister children and their Indian friends watched the putt-putting craft round the point into Sitka Sound. Then it headed out toward a group of distant islands.

Bitter disappointment showed on the faces of Rossy and Beth. Twice in a short time they had seen their stolen boat, yet had been powerless to get it or catch the thief!

"We'll look for him again tomorrow," Pete declared as they descended the steps from the site of the old Baranof castle.

"Please come visit us," Beth said as she squeezed Pam's hand. "We'd like you to meet our parents."

The Hollisters promised to do this, then waved good-by and returned to the hotel.

The invitation excited the younger Hollisters when they heard about it at breakfast in the coffee shop next morning.

"Then I can play with Sasha!" Sue said delightedly.

Mrs. Hollister and Aunt Marge wanted to see an exhibit of native art in one of the stores, while Uncle

Russ planned to make sketches in the town. They gave permission for the children to visit the Indians.

The cousins trooped down the street to the house where the Kindues lived. When they stopped in front of the unpainted small frame building, Sue looked disappointed. "I thought Indians up here lived in wigwams," she said.

"Oh no," Pam informed her. "The Northwest Indians live in wooden houses."

At that moment Beth opened the door. Rossy was behind her. They ran down a short flight of wooden steps to greet the callers, then invited them inside. Ushered into the living room of the house, the Hollisters noticed that the furniture was plain and well worn.

"I'll call Mother and Daddy," Beth said and hurried off.

Rossy chatted with the visitors until his parents appeared. Mr. Kindue was a short man with jet black hair, high cheekbones, and a serene face. His wife was stout and had a pretty smile. She wore a red and white apron.

"Thank you for helping our children look for their boat," Mrs. Kindue said as she shook hands. Her husband wished them success because his son and daughter had been looking forward to the Salmon Derby for a whole year.

"Perhaps," Pam replied smiling, "while we're helping you locate your missing boat, you can help us find a mysterious old totem pole."

The Kindues listened intently as Pam told of their quest. Mr. Kindue said that he was a Tlingit Indian and his wife a Haida. Between them they knew many strange stories of the southeast Alaskan coast.

They sat quietly for several seconds, thinking, then Mrs. Kindue said, "I remember hearing a story something like that."

"About the raven totem?" Pam queried, excitedly.

"Yes. Someone hid it on an island near Sitka."

"Crickets!" Pete exclaimed. "Maybe Farley heard the same story!"

"Sure," Ricky said. "That's where he was going last night—to look for the raven totem!"

Little Sue, who was not so interested in this as the older children, suddenly said, "Mrs. Kindly, does your family have front Indian names?"

The woman laughed. "Indeed we do. Rossy's is Dow-chun. And our Beth has the Indian name of Kahsahn."

"Don't forget me, Mama," Sasha spoke up. "I'm Doo-oo."

"Oh, how pretty!" Holly said, delighted by the pleasant sounds.

"We use American names most of the time," Rossy said. "Dad's is Walter and Mother's is Genevieve."

"And we do American work," Mr. Kindue told the visitors with a chuckle. "I'm a carpenter. Mama makes Tlingit dolls to sell."

"That must be fun," Holly remarked.

"It is," the Indian woman said. "But I couldn't manage without the help of my daughters."

At this point Mr. Kindue excused himself, saying he had to go to work.

The girls immediately became absorbed in a conversation about doll-making. Seeing this, Pete leaned close to Rossy and beckoned Ricky and Teddy to his side. "Listen, fellows, while the girls are talking about dolls, suppose we go looking for Abalone Farley. And we might even find the totem pole!"

"But we have no boat," Rossy reminded him.

"Perhaps we can borrow one," Pete said. "Does Mr. Carr own a boat?"

"Yes," Rossy answered. "I wonder if he'd lend it to us."

Pete said the hotel owner had been very nice to them. If they told him the circumstances, perhaps he would lend his boat for the day.

"And we can fish at the same time!" the Indian boy declared, his face brightening at the idea.

Rossy said that the owner of a small restaurant nearby needed a few salmon for the next day's menu. "He'll pay a good price for fresh fish." The Indian boy grinned.

"Good! We'll catch a lot!" Ricky said confidently.

Rossy told his mother of their plan. "Fine," she said. "I hope you catch a few salmon and find our boat, too."

The four companions lost no time. They descended the front steps in leaps and raced toward the hotel.

When Mr. Carr heard their story, he gladly offered his boat for the day.

"The gas tank is full," he said, "and if you need more fishing equipment, help yourself to some gear in the closet at the back of the lobby."

Rossy raced back home to get his fishing line and the Hollister boys each took a pole from the closet. A few minutes later they met in front of the hotel. In addition to his pole, Rossy carried a bucket half filled with water. In it Ricky saw a small package.

"What's that?" he asked.

"Frozen herring," Rossy replied. "We use them for bait."

"All aboard," Teddy called out, and the boys hurried toward the dock where Mr. Carr's motorboat was moored.

The girls, meanwhile, were still deep in talk about Indian dolls. "I'd love to see the ones you make," Pam told Mrs. Kindue.

The woman led her visitors into a little glassed-in sun porch which led off the living room. In it was a sewing machine and a table on which lay bits of material. In a cardboard box nearby were half a dozen dolls, all of the same kind.

"This is Mother's specialty," Beth said, holding one up. "This doll is called Wan-wa-shaw. In Tlingit that means little sailor girl."

"How cute!" Holly declared as she reached out to take the toy. It was about ten inches tall and was dressed in a black wool skirt and red-fringed jacket.

They worked carefully on the dolls.

"The body is so soft!" Holly said as she passed the doll to Sue.

"That's because it's made of genuine deerskin," Mrs. Kindue gave as the reason.

Sue touched the boots on each of the doll's feet. They also were made of deerskin, with a border of red wool decorated with yellow and green beads.

"I think the hair is pretty, too," Jean remarked. It was jet black and made of wool, which hung down in two long pigtails over the shoulders.

Pam said she was intrigued mostly with the painted face. "The doll looks happy," she said.

At this Beth chuckled. "I help Mother paint the faces," she said.

Wan-wa-shaw, with her reindeer-skin face, had much the same coloring as the Indian children. Her nose was really two dots and the little red mouth was very similar to Sasha's. Dark brows were painted above two large and luminous eyes.

"We have a few more doll faces to paint," Mrs. Kindue said, "before we take this batch to the souvenir shop to be sold."

"Please may we help?" Holly asked.

"Well," Mrs. Kindue said kindly, "perhaps you should practice painting doll faces on paper before you work on the deerskin."

"I'd love to try," Pam said.

In a few moments the Indian woman produced paints, brushes, and pieces of paper. The Hollister girls began to work. Pam and Jean did very well on their first try, especially Jean. Uncle Russ had shown his daughter how to draw pictures, so it was no wonder that her effort was better than Holly's and Sue's.

After each girl had tried several times, Mrs. Kindue gave permission for all except Sue to paint on the deerskin faces. Sue's doll faces continued to look like happy pixies instead of Indian girls, but this did not bother her.

As the older children carefully worked on the doll faces, Sue and Sasha went off to sit in a corner with their own paints and brushes. They were extremely quiet for several minutes.

"What are you up to?" Mrs. Kindue asked.

"This!" Sue declared.

She held her hands in the air. On each fingernail was painted a little pixie face.

"Me too," said Sasha as she showed her hands.

The others laughed, then Mrs. Kindue hurried Sue and Sasha out of the room to wash the paint off before it dried.

The doll-painting project went on for another hour. When two dozen of the lovely souvenirs had been completed, Beth's mother said, "Let's take these to the shop and see if we can sell them."

The Indian woman covered the top of the carton with tissue paper and put it under her arm. She and the girls left the house and walked to the main street, where the shop was located. Inside it a pleasant, gray-haired woman greeted them.

"I have more dolls for you today," Mrs. Kindue said.

"Oh fine!" replied the woman as she took the box and placed it on the counter. "May I tell my customers that these were made entirely by Indians?"

Pam and Mrs. Kindue exchanged glances. They would have to tell the truth, of course.

"No," the Indian woman answered, "these Hollister girls helped me paint the faces."

"Oh, I'm sorry—" came the reply.

CHAPTER 13

THE STOLEN BOAT

THE owner of the souvenir shop suddenly noticed the look of dismay on Pam's face.

"Oh, don't worry," the woman said quickly. "I was about to say I'm sorry you didn't bring me more of such pretty dolls to sell."

Pam was relieved. "You like them?"

"I think they're lovely," the woman replied.

As she handed Mrs. Kindue money for the toys, she said that it did not matter who had painted the faces, just so long as the clothes and the bodies of the dolls had been made by Alaskan Indians.

During all this time the boys had been enjoying themselves immensely. Rossy sat in the stern of Mr. Carr's speedy outboard motorboat, one hand on the tiller. Ricky and Teddy were in the middle seat, while Pete occupied the bow.

As the wind whipped through their hair, the boys glanced back over the churning white wake to see the docks of Sitka growing smaller in the distance. Finally Rossy stopped the motor.

"I'll show you how to bait the lines for trolling," he told the others.

The Indian boy opened his fishing kit and pulled out four shiny spinners. He attached these to the lines, then baited the hooks with the small herring. By this time the frozen fish had thawed enough to be handled separately. After the boys had put their lines in the water, Rossy started the boat again. Now it putt-putted along slowly.

"It's a good time to fish," the Indian said, "because the tide is coming in." He explained that the salmon fed either at high or at low tide, and added, "We'll head toward old Sitka. I know a good fishing spot there."

Questioned by Pete about old Sitka, Rossy said that this was the place where the Russian explorers had built their first fort. After it had been destroyed by fire, they moved to the present site of the town.

Chugging slowly past several islands, Pete and the others wondered if any of these held the missing mysterious old totem. But first in importance, they realized, was to find the Kindue's missing boat. As they trolled, the boys kept a sharp lookout for it.

Presently Ricky felt a tug on his line. "Hey! I've got something!" As he reeled in, a fish broke the surface of the water and flopped in the air.

"Keep your line taut," Rossy advised. "I think it's a bass."

Ricky's face was so flushed with excitement that his freckles stood out clearer than ever. He brought his catch alongside, and Rossy scooped it up with a large net. Pete unhooked the fish as it lay in the bottom of the boat.

"That's a small one, about four pounds," Rossy announced. "We'll throw him back in."

"What!" Ricky said in consternation. "Why back in Shoreham that would be a big one!"

"Not here," Rossy told him, grinning. He nodded to Pete to flip the bass back into the water.

"Don't be disappointed, Ricky," the Indian boy said. "You'll catch a big one yet."

Teddy was looking up at a snow-capped peak in the distance when he felt his line jerk. He gave it a tug to set the hook. Then his pole bent.

Rossy stopped the motor. "You've got a big one there, Teddy. I believe it's a king salmon."

Teddy's line moved back and forth as the fish fought to free itself. The boy's arms ached, but he reeled in little by little. Finally they all saw a glint of silver in the water beside their boat.

"A king," Rossy said happily.

"What a beauty!" Pete cried, as Rossy handed him the net to scoop up the fish. "Crickets! This is heavy!"

He swung the catch into the bottom of the boat. The big fish flopped about ferociously until Rossy stunned it with a short stick.

Teddy had to use both hands to hold up his prize for the others to see.

"Yikes!" Ricky chortled. "How much does that weigh, Rossy?"

"About thirty pounds. Fine catch!"

"What a beauty!"

"I'm giving it to you, Rossy," Teddy said. "Keep it or sell it to the restaurant man if you like."

"Thanks, Teddy."

Pete declared this should be a fine spot in which to fish during the Derby.

"It's one of the best," Rossy said. But he looked worried as he added, "I'm afraid Beth and I will have to pass up the Derby this year."

"Maybe not," Pete said encouragingly. "We'll keep looking for your boat." Then he added, "Say, who's that fisherman over there?"

Pete pointed toward a large motorboat coming up between them and an island not far offshore. Two long poles extended out from either side of the boat.

Rossy turned to look and his face brightened. "That's Mr. Hoffman. He's my schoolteacher in the winter. During vacation time he's a commercial fisherman.

"Hi, Mr. Hoffman!" Rossy called as he drew closer.

"Hello, Rossy. How's everything today?"

"Not bad," he said and introduced his friends. "We got a good king. But someone stole my motorboat. We won't be able to fish in the Derby."

Mr. Hoffman expressed his sympathy and said he would be on the lookout for the boat. After his pupil had described the thief in detail, the teacher said, "I saw someone answering that description only half an hour ago."

Pete's heart thumped with excitement. "Where did he go, Mr. Hoffman?"

The teacher pointed in the direction of Mount Annahootz, adding, "That might have been your boat he was running, Rossy."

"We'll go after it right away," the boy replied. Then he turned to the others. "Let's stow the gear and go full speed ahead."

The Hollisters pulled in their lines. Rossy advanced the gas until the motor roared, sending them northward over the glittering water in the direction of the towering, snow-capped peak.

They circled the two islands on their left. But though the boys kept a sharp watch on the shore lines of them, they failed to see the Kindues' boat.

"I guess the fellow had too much of a head start," Teddy remarked as they sped past a smaller island.

"What's this one called?" Pete asked.

"Fox Island. A Haida Indian had a fox farm here at one time, but it's abandoned now."

Just as Rossy spoke, the motor stopped suddenly and the boat bobbed in the waves. The boy put his hand on the casing covering the motor. "Too hot. I guess it overheated."

"Maybe we can start it again," Pete said. Having had experience with motorboats on Pine Lake, he began to tinker with the outboard. He tried again and again to start the engine but without success.

"I guess you're right," he said. "We'll have to wait for it to cool off."

As they waited, however, the wind grew stronger

and dark clouds scudded in front of the sun. Now the waters looked leaden and grew rougher.

"We're drifting closer to the island," Pete remarked.

Rossy said this was probably a good idea. They could beach the boat and look around for a while. A few moments later the bow touched the rocky shore. The boys hopped out, tilted the outboard up, then pulled the boat up on a pebbly strip between two boulders.

"Are there any foxes around?" Ricky asked.

"No. Not any more."

Ricky looked disappointed. "Well, let's look for the totem pole anyway."

The boys made their way along the craggy shore line. But their progress was slowed by boggy ground covered with moss and gnarled tree roots.

"This kind of growth is called *muskeg* in Alaska," Rossy said, as the companions pressed on doggedly.

Finally they came to a huge fallen tree. The top half of it lay in the water. Ricky clambered over it first and called from the other side:

"Hey fellows! I see a boat!"

"Where?" Pete asked, hurrying to his brother's side.

"Over there! Look!" Ricky pointed to a cove where the bow of a red boat was visible among low hanging limbs.

Rossy stood stock-still for a moment. "The flag—the flag of Alaska. I see it!"

Now all four boys ran along the beach, scrambling over roots and boulders.

"It *is* our boat!" Rossy cried out as they reached it. "Let's take it!"

The anchor had been thrown out over a log. Quickly Rossy put it into the boat. The boys climbed in and shoved off.

"I hope the motor works," said Pete.

Rossy started it. At first the engine sputtered, then vibrated into a steady hum as he backed the boat far out into the water.

"Boy oh boy!" Ricky cried gleefully. Then he sobered. "Do you suppose Abalone Farley is on the island?"

"Sure," Rossy replied. "And he won't be able to get away. We'll tell the police to pick him up."

"Say," said Pete worriedly, "Farley may help himself to Mr. Carr's boat! The engine will be cool by this time."

"He won't if we get there first," Rossy answered determinedly, and gave his craft full power.

In a few minutes he reached the spot where they had left the boat. It was still there!

"Let's tow it," Rossy suggested.

The boys tied a rope from its bow to the stern of Rossy's motorboat and started off.

"Look at those black clouds!" Teddy pointed to the sullen sky.

"We'd better hurry," Ricky advised worriedly.

Rossy increased the speed of his craft. It knifed

through the water with the waves slapping against the hull. The wind grew stronger, blowing whitecaps like suds over the wave tops.

"Do you suppose we can make it back to Sitka?" Pete asked anxiously.

CHAPTER 14

AN ESKIMO YO-YO

WHILE the boys had been having their amazing adventure on Fox Island and were now racing across the storm-swept channel, their sisters were busy in Sitka. After leaving the shop where the dolls were sold, Mrs. Kindue had said she must return home with Sasha.

"Beth, why don't you show the Hollisters some more of the famous places in town?"

The Indian girl turned to her friends and asked, "Have you been inside St. Michael's Cathedral?"

"No," Jean replied. "Is that the church overlooking the main street?"

Beth nodded, saying that the cathedral was a famous landmark. The early settlers had built it of logs in the shape of a Greek cross and covered it with clapboards.

"It's been standing there since 1844," she said.

"Let's go see it," Pam proposed.

Mrs. Kindue departed with Sasha, leaving the other girls to walk down the street toward the unusual-looking church.

Sue gazed up at the dome beneath the towering

spire and remarked, "It looks just like an upside-down ice-cream cone." The others smiled.

As they approached the front of the edifice, Jean said, "We don't see many churches like this in our country."

Several sight-seers had gathered there, and a woman wearing a white nurse's uniform told the girls the doors would be open in a few minutes. Just then a man wearing black robes and a long reddish beard ushered the visitors inside.

The first thing to catch Pam's eye was an ornate golden chandelier which hung from the ceiling before a beautiful altar. "How lovely!" she said softly. Then her eyes roved over the six large oil paintings, three on either side of the altar. "Beautiful," she thought.

Sue tugged at her sister's hand and Pam bent over. "Where do the people sit?" the little girl whispered.

For the first time Pam became aware that there were no pews in the church. The woman in white overheard the question.

"The worshipers in this cathedral remain standing when not kneeling in prayer. This was the custom in all ancient Russian churches."

The woman beckoned the girls to follow her. Leading them to the left, she stopped in front of a smaller altar. Over it was a Madonna and Child of exquisite beauty. The faces were painted in oils, but the halos were made of pure beaten gold.

"This is the Sitka Madonna," she told them. "It's very famous."

Nearby was a book for visitors to sign. When the children had written their names, they left the church quietly. Once outside, the woman in the white uniform spoke to them again.

"I'm Mrs. Bonney," she said and the girls introduced themselves.

"Are you a nurse?" Pam asked.

Mrs. Bonney said yes. She served at Mt. Edgecumbe Hospital.

"Do you help little Eskimos and Indians to get well?" Holly asked her.

Mrs. Bonney smiled and said she did her best.

"Oh, I'd love to see an Eskimo!" Sue declared with a giggle. "Do they wear their furs to bed, Mrs. Bonney?"

The woman laughed and said that Eskimo and Indian children at the hospital dressed much the same as the Hollisters. Then she added, "How would you girls like to visit the hospital with me?"

"We'd love to!" Jean said.

Mrs. Bonney told them she was going to catch the next ferryboat which crossed the channel to the island on which the hospital was located. "You may come with me now if you like," she added.

Pam said she would tell her mother and raced ahead of the others. Entering the hotel, she found Mrs. Hollister about to set out with Aunt Marge on a shopping tour. The two women came outside to meet the nurse and gave permission for the girls to go with her.

As Mrs. Bonney and the girls walked toward the waterfront, Holly and Sue held the woman's hands.

"Hurray! We're going to see the Eskimos!" Sue sang over and over.

"Here comes the ferryboat now," Mrs. Bonney said.

The craft was small by comparison with ferryboats the Hollister children had seen. It was almost all cabin. As it came closer to the dock, the girls could see the faces of many passengers looking out the windows. After the ferry had been made fast to the mooring, the people trooped out. Mrs. Bonney said most of them were Indians who worked at the hospital.

"Come now and stick close to me," she went on. "I don't want to lose any of you girls." She chuckled.

They followed her down a long covered wooden ramp. But Jean lagged behind to watch a small airplane glide in and land on the water at the nearby seaplane basin.

"Come on, Jean!" Holly urged, turning around and beckoning to her cousin.

"I'll be right there!"

Jean was fascinated by the whirling propeller as the airplane moved slowly over the water to the side of a dock.

"I wonder who's in it," she thought.

As the girl watched, a young man stepped out. He was followed by a woman who held a small baby in her arms.

"What a lovely flying family!" the girl said to herself. "Maybe Daddy would like to sketch them."

"Jean! Hurry!" Holly called out. "The boat'll go without you!"

Just then the engines of the ferry rumbled louder. Jean ended her daydreaming abruptly and raced toward the boat. Everyone was aboard except her.

"Wait! Please!" she cried to the man who was about to cast off a stout line. Her legs flew as she ran toward the boat. The fellow reached over to the dock and took Jean by the hand, helping her to leap onto the ferryboat.

"You nearly had to swim," he said, grinning.

"Oh, thank you," Jean said, panting.

The ride across the channel was a short one and soon the girls found themselves on the island. Now they could see the hospital buildings more clearly. Mrs. Bonney led them along a sidewalk skirting several white structures which gleamed in the sun.

"Are all the poor little Eskimos sick?" Holly asked the nurse.

"Not all of them," Mrs. Bonney replied. "Many are almost well and are now regaining their strength. These are the ones we'll visit."

"Look!" the nurse said. "There are some little Eskimos now."

She pointed up to a row of windows on the third floor of one of the buildings. The round-faced Eskimo children peered down at the Hollisters and Beth. Pam waved and the little patients waved back.

"Are those the ones we're going to visit?" Jean asked.

"Yes. Follow me."

Mrs. Bonney led the girls up a flight of concrete steps and entered the hospital building. They took an elevator to the third floor and walked down a long corridor.

"Step right inside this ward," Mrs. Bonney directed.

It was filled with smiling, chubby children. Their dark eyes squinted to slits when they smiled. All had pearly white teeth and straight black hair.

Some of the young patients were seated on their beds, playing games. Others were busy at little tables, coloring picture books. In one corner a boy was playing a tune on a toy piano.

"Are you Eskimos?" Sue blurted out.

The children looked at one another and grinned. Then they nodded their heads vigorously. It took only a few minutes for the Hollister girls and Beth to make friends with the Eskimos.

Holly talked to one girl with bright eyes and dimples. "Did your father ever catch a walrus?" she asked.

The little Eskimo girl giggled and said yes. She herself had caught a baby one!

"Did you keep it for a pet?"

"Yes. But it grew too big and I let it go back into the sea."

Just then another girl about Pam's age showed them

a curious Eskimo toy. Two fur balls were suspended at the end of leather thongs.

"What do you call that?" Pam asked, as Beth looked on.

"An Eskimo yo-yo."

"How does it work?"

The Eskimo girl twirled one of the balls in one direction, then spun the second in an opposite circle. Skillfully she kept the two balls rotating in opposite directions.

"Oh, that looks like fun!" Jean exclaimed. "May I try it, please?"

"Of course." The smiling girl handed the yo-yo to her.

As Jean took the Eskimo toy in her hands, Mrs. Bonney beckoned to five little native girls.

"Where are they going?" Sue asked.

The girl with the yo-yo said, "It's a surprise."

Jean now tried to twirl the two fur balls. She started one spinning nicely. When she set the other one in motion, *plop!* The fur hit Beth on the nose. The rest of the children laughed.

Just after everyone had taken a turn at the new game, Mrs. Bonney returned with the five little Eskimo girls. They were dressed in nurses' uniforms and caps that fit them perfectly. On the front of their outfits they wore red crosses.

"Oh, how cute!" Jean declared.

Mrs. Bonney explained that the Eskimo children

"One, two, three, kick!"

had made these outfits themselves. They would put on a little show for the Hollisters.

The Eskimo "nurses" grinned shyly, then formed a line as if for marching. Each girl grasped the one in front about the waist. The boy at the piano played a lively tune, and the five girls started to dance. Mrs. Bonney called out:

"One, two, three, kick!"

Sue giggled and started to do the same little routine herself. One of the Eskimo girls waved for her to join the dance, so Sue cavorted about with them.

When the dance was over, Mrs. Bonney said she had another surprise for the visitors. She ordered them to close their eyes and open their hands. Then she pressed something into each one.

"Now open your eyes!"

In the girls' palms lay tiny walruses carved from ivory tusk. The nurse explained that the father of one of the little patients had made them. He had sent the souvenirs to the hospital to be used as gifts.

"Oh, thank you so much!" said Pam and the others. The nurse then said it was time for them to leave.

"May we rub noses good-by?" Holly asked. She had heard that rubbing noses was the same as kissing among the Eskimos.

Mrs. Bonney said they might do this, and the little girls rubbed noses vigorously, then waved good-by.

"Now you have seen real Eskimos," Mrs. Bonney said laughingly as they left the building. She glanced up at the sky. "Look," the nurse went on, "a storm is coming from the north now. It must be from Eskimo-land."

As the little group walked toward the water, the wind rose and the waves in the channel grew choppy. By the time the Hollister girls and their friends reached the ferryboat dock, the wind was howling.

"Oh dear," Jean said, looking a little worried. "I hope we can get back safely."

Mrs. Bonney assured her that the ferry had made many trips in worse weather than this. When everyone was aboard, the boat started across the channel.

Pam stood up to gaze at the wild beauty of the storm as it ripped across the open water. As they neared Sitka she cried to the others:

"Come here quick! Look!"

All the girls gazed out the windows. Two motorboats, one towing the other, were approaching the Sitka dock.

"Pete and the rest of the boys are in the front boat!" Pam exclaimed.

"And the boat is ours!" Beth yelled.

The Indian girl did not know whether to laugh or weep with joy.

"They've found our motorboat!" she sobbed. "Now we can enter the Salmon Derby!"

CHAPTER 15

AN ALASKAN CONTEST

MRS. Bonney said good-by to the girls, who hurried off the ferry and rushed to where the four boys were docking the motorboats.

Rossy stepped out first, lugging the big salmon. Quickly the story of the boys' adventure was told.

"Abalone Farley is probably on Fox Island," Pete said. "We'll notify the police."

All this time Beth had been staring at the Kindues' motorboat, as if she could not believe the family's good fortune. "My father and mother will be so happy," she said.

Before the Indian children went off to notify Chief Harris, Rossy said, "Beth and I will be entering the Salmon Derby. It starts tomorrow at seven. I wish I could invite you all but only four can go. Pete and Pam, will you join us?"

The Hollister children were thrilled and said they would be glad to.

"We'll meet you at the dock," Pete answered.

The Hollisters went to their hotel. At once Pete spoke to Mr. Carr and thanked him for the use of his boat and tackle, then told him how the motor had failed.

"I think the fuel line is clogged," Mr. Carr said. "Don't worry about that! I'll fix it in a jiffy tomorrow."

He was amazed to learn how the children had recovered the stolen boat. "I hope the thief is rounded up soon. And I'm glad the Indian children will be able to participate in the Derby."

"My sister Pam and I are going with them," Pete said. "Will you please awaken me at six, Mr. Carr? And Pam too. We don't want to be late for the Derby."

Mr. Carr said he would, and added, "The whole town will be up and about at that time. You'll hear them!"

The hotel man told the children that the Salmon Derby was like Christmas, New Year's and Fourth of July all put together. Hardly anybody in town worked during the three-day event.

"We'll all be out trying to catch the biggest fish. I'll be there too!" he said, chuckling.

Next morning, shortly before six, the entire family was awakened by the noise of talking and bustling in the streets.

"Mr. Carr was right," Pete thought as he dressed quickly.

When the phone at Pete's bedside tinkled, the boy picked it up. "Good morning," said the clerk. "I hope you're all set to catch a whopper today."

"Oh thanks," Pete replied, grinning.

"I'll phone your sister now," the clerk said.

Since everyone was awake, the whole Hollister family had an early breakfast in the hotel dining room. At a quarter to seven Pete and Pam said good-by to the others, grinning broadly.

"Catch a little minnow for me," Uncle Russ called teasingly.

When Pete and Pam reached the docks, they gasped to see the activity before them. The waterfront was alive with people and purring motorboats.

"Hi!" Rossy said, as he and Beth greeted the Hollisters. "Hop in. We're all set to go."

Dozens of craft entering the Derby milled about in the water of the boat basin, awaiting the official whistle to send them on their way.

"Oh, isn't this thrilling!" Pam exclaimed.

Promptly at seven came a loud blast. Cheers filled the air. Motors roared and the colorful flotilla scattered north and south. Some boats headed for Silver Bay. Others, including Rossy's, streaked northward toward old Sitka.

A few of the craft, speedier than the eighteen-horsepower strength of the Kindues' motorboat, passed the four voyagers. Others dropped behind them.

While Rossy was busy at the tiller, Pete baited the hooks. As he attached a frozen herring to Beth's line, she cried out, "Look! Porpoises!"

Not far from their boat three of the sleek creatures dipped in and out of the water with graceful rhythm.

Rossy grinned. "That means good luck!"

"Hop in. We're all set to go."

"I hope so!" Pete shouted exultantly.

The Hollisters had seen porpoises in Florida, but had no idea that the jolly mammals appeared so far north.

"Oh yes," Beth replied to Pam's comment on this above the noise of the throbbing motor. She explained that in the spring, finback whales were to be seen in Sitka Sound. "Sometimes big sperm whales too."

"And plenty of seals and sea lions," Rossy added.

As the motorboat neared the fishing spot they had chosen, conversation turned to the species of salmon they might catch.

"The prize goes to the largest king or Chinook," Beth told the Hollisters.

"Are there other kinds, too?" Pam asked.

Rossy said yes, four other varieties. These were the humpback, or pink salmon; the dog salmon, or chum; the cohoe, or silver salmon, and the sockeye, or red.

Pete grinned broadly and looked into the deep water. "Please, Mr. Chinook, grab my line!"

Now, as the boats fanned out, Rossy cut the motor to trolling speed, and the lines were payed out into the cold water.

"Set your drags loose," Rossy directed the Hollisters. "If a big one should strike, then he won't break your line."

Soon they reached the spot where the large salmon had been caught the day before. As Rossy steered the boat a hundred yards from the shore of Fox Island,

Pam noticed that the occupants of an adjoining motor-boat were pulling aboard a large fish.

"That's a beauty!" Rossy said. "I hope we get one as large."

Pam was enjoying the beauty of the scenery as well as the thrill of the contest. She gazed at the island's spruce and cedar forest where a giant eagle soared at treetop level. Then her mind turned to Abalone Farley. Had he been caught?

Just then Pam's glance fell on five little ducks bobbing in the water. "What do you call them, Beth?" she asked.

The Indian girl said they were dovekies and pronounced it doe-vee-kie. They were friendly birds, she said, which dived down to catch small fish. Just then all five dovekies disappeared. At the same moment Pam felt a tug on her line.

"You've caught something!" Rossy exclaimed. "Jerk your pole!"

Pam did as instructed. The top of her pole vibrated as the fish tried to get away.

"Hold your pole up high!" Beth told her.

The fish raced one way, then the other, as Pam reeled in the line steadily. All at once there was a silver flash along the side of the boat. Rossy dipped his net into the water, then said:

"Look, Pam, you've caught it by the tail!"

None of the children had ever seen such a thing before. The hook was embedded in the king salmon behind the dorsal fin.

"Easy now, or we may not get him," the Indian boy cautioned. But, with a quick movement, he netted the fish and dropped it inside the boat.

Pam's hands shook with excitement. "Is it a prize winner?"

Rossy chuckled. "Not quite, Pam. But it's a good start. I'd say this one weighs twenty-five pounds."

After Pete had unhooked the catch and rebaited the line, the fishermen continued their trolling. Rossy pointed to a spot between two distant islands and told his guests that the Russian ship *Neva* had sunk there in 1780.

"Crickets!" cried Pete. "17—oops!" His fishing pole was almost pulled from his hands. The boy's palms stung from the friction.

"Hang on!" Rossy cried. The Indian boy stopped the motor and moved over to stand by his friend. "It's either a baby whale or a giant king! Careful how you play it, Pete."

Several nearby boats also stopped to watch the battle between Pete and the fish. It ranged back and forth, diving now and then for deeper water.

As minutes went by, Pete's arms grew tired and he felt a numbness in his fingers. But according to the rules of the Derby, no one could help him reel in his catch.

Pete grinned as he kept reeling in. "This baby must weigh half a ton!"

Finally a silver stripe gleamed underwater twenty feet from the boat.

"It *is* a king!" Rossy shouted. "And a granddaddy, too! Hold on, Pete!"

In a final effort, the fish lunged to get beneath the boat, but Pete held it steady. Its huge tail fanned tiredly as the salmon was pulled alongside and Rossy scooped it up with the net.

Plop! The huge fish landed in the bottom of the boat and flopped about wildly.

Pam shrieked with mingled fear and amazement. "Will it bite us?"

"Now, now," Rossy assured her as he quickly clubbed the monstrous fish.

Pete sat down and let his arms hang limply over his knees. "How much would you say it weighs, Rossy?"

"Over seventy pounds."

"Then it might win a prize?" Pam asked excitedly. The Indian children grinned and said yes. They were happy that Pete had done so well.

"I think we ought to take this back to Sitka before we do any more fishing." Rossy grinned. "It takes up a lot of room in the boat."

As they neared the boat basin, Pam said, "While we're here, let's ask about Farley." The others agreed. All wanted to know if the thief had been captured.

After they reached the dock, Pete first had his fish weighed. The official in charge lifted his eyebrows as the needle on the scale reached seventy-five pounds.

"This may be the largest for the day," he said, smiling. "Are you going out again?"

"Oh yes," Rossy replied hurriedly. "A little later."

Leaving Pete's catch with the Derby official, the four children started for the police station. On the way they met Russ Hollister. When he heard about the fish, the cartoonist gave a low whistle. "I'm certainly going to sketch it and use the Derby in a strip of pictures," he said.

Pam told him where the children were heading and Uncle Russ said he would go along. "I'd like to find out about that rascal myself," he said.

When they reached headquarters, the group found Chief Harris on duty. After greeting them, he said, "You children must have a sixth sense, coming here. We had no trace of Abalone Farley until ten minutes ago. Then one of my men picked up a clue."

"You know where he is?" Pete asked excitedly.

"Not exactly. But a fisherman told the officer he had rescued a man from Fox Island last night and put him on the mainland several miles from Sitka. The fellow said his boat had been stolen."

"By us." Pete grinned. "Did the description fit Farley?"

"It sure did. And I'm going after him right away," the officer answered. "If I find he's around, I'll send a posse after him. Want to come along?"

"Crickets! Do I?" Pete cried out. "How are we going? By speedboat?"

"No, by plane."

Chief Harris telephoned a pilot who often helped him. They would meet him at the seaplane basin in ten minutes.

"But the plane is only a single-motored craft with five seats," the officer said.

Rossy spoke up at once. "Oh, Beth and I couldn't ride along. We're going out fishing again," he told the chief.

The Indian boy and his sister said good-by and hurried back to their boat. Uncle Russ phoned a message to the hotel, informing the rest of the family where he, Pete, and Pam were going. Then the three Hollisters hurried to the seaplane basin with Chief Harris.

On the way he said, "When that fisherman picked up Farley, he had a long package, like a pole, all wrapped up in burlap. He carried it along."

Pete and Pam exchanged glances. Could this be the mystery totem pole? Their hearts sank at the thought.

Aloud Pam said, "We *must* find Abalone Farley!"

When they reached the shore, Chief Harris introduced the Hollisters to the pilot, a young man named Randy. He had the motor warmed up and was ready to fly. The four passengers climbed in.

Randy taxied out into the channel. After finding a stretch of water clear of fishing boats, he took off. Then he flew over the treetops close to the shore. Fifteen minutes later, Chief Harris said tensely, "We're coming to the spot where the fisherman let Farley off."

The Hollister children's hearts beat wildly.

CHAPTER 16

THE RAVEN'S HEAD

As THE pilot flew low, Pam shouted, "There he is!" In a tiny cove a man had been visible for a moment. "Oh, he's gone into the woods!"

Randy flew back and forth over the area, but no one could be seen in the heavy woodland which spread like a tufted carpet from the snow-capped peak down to the lapping water.

"We'd better land," Chief Harris said. "If that man is not Farley, we'll soon find out. If he is, he'll probably run away. Then I'll send for the posse."

The pilot brought the seaplane down and taxied to the shore. No one met them. The chief shouted for the man they had seen to come to the waterfront. Still the fellow did not appear.

"It must have been Farley," Pam insisted. "Look over there."

Tucked under a low-hanging tree was a quantity of fresh burlap.

Chief Harris nodded. "You're right. It's what was wrapped around the thing he was carrying."

"The mystery totem," Pam said. "Oh, we must find it."

155

"We'll start out as soon as I call headquarters," the officer told her.

Randy picked up his microphone and relayed the message that they wanted to surround the fugitive.

"A posse will be here by speedboat as soon as possible, Chief," Randy said.

He brought the plane alongside a stout log which extended into the water. Pete, Pam, Uncle Russ, and the chief stepped out onto it and walked ashore. Randy would remain with the plane until they returned.

"I see the fellow's tracks right here," Uncle Russ said, pointing the way. Footprints were clearly visible in the spongy muskeg.

Following the trail, the four climbed up to an outcropping of rock. There was a deep, narrow gouge in the undergrowth from a heavy object being dragged across it. On a ledge Pam noticed something which made her pulse throb. Small scrapings of wood clung to the jagged edges of the rocks.

"Farley is carrying the totem with him!" Pete exclaimed.

"He couldn't have left a clearer trail with a tractor!" Uncle Russ remarked wryly as they climbed farther up the slope.

As the chase went on, the chief began to pant and Uncle Russ mopped his forehead with a handkerchief. Pete and Pam ranged ahead of the men, but promised to be careful.

When they came to the roots of a gnarled, fallen

tree which blocked their path, Pete reached back to take Pam's hand. Her fingers were moist from exertion and she slipped from her brother's grip.

"Oh!" she cried out, pitching backward.

Her left leg jammed between the roots and the rotted tree trunk. Pete sprang quickly to her side. "Are you all right, Sis?"

"I—I guess so," the girl said as she pulled her leg out of the crevice.

"Does it hurt?"

"A little," Pam replied, wincing. "But I guess I can make it, Pete."

By now Uncle Russ and the chief had caught up to them.

"Thank goodness, you didn't break your leg," the chief said as he examined Pam's bruised shin. Then he added, "Farley can't be too far ahead of us."

Bravely, Pam continued on, with Pete helping her over the rougher spots. The slope grew steeper. If Farley were somewhere ahead, Pete reasoned, he must be tiring. Pressing forward eagerly, the boy climbed through a dense thicket. Suddenly he stumbled upon what he thought was a stump. Even in the gloom of the forest canopy he could see that there were colors on it.

"A totem!" the boy cried out. "Pam, we've found it!"

His sister limped up. "Pete," she said, "it's only the bottom half of a totem pole. Look!"

Her guess was confirmed by the chief and Uncle

Russ. It was the lower half of a pole which had rotted through and broken off.

"Oh dear," Pam murmured. "If that's the totem pole we're looking for, the top half must contain the secret hiding place, or Farley wouldn't have left this!"

A quick examination of the carved figures revealed that this indeed was the mystery totem pole. Pete went over it again. There was no secret hiding place nor was there a message on any part of it.

The idea of success being only a short distance ahead of them spurred Pete to renewed effort. A surge of strength came to his tiring legs and he scrambled up the hillside with fresh vigor.

All at once he stopped and listened, then called back, "I hear Farley. He's not far ahead of us!"

Uncle Russ was directly behind Pete. He joined the lad and they climbed side by side.

"There! I see him now!" Uncle Russ said, and shouted, "Stop, thief! Stop in the name of the law!"

Pete and his uncle gazed up a steep bluff to see Farley standing there with a short log raised over his head.

"The raven totem!" Pete said.

"Yes!" came a thin, whining voice. "And if you want the thing so badly, here it is!"

Farley hurled the wooden pole down at his pursuers. Pete and his uncle ducked just in time. The raven's head crashed against a tree behind them.

As the boy ran to retrieve it, Farley started off again.

"The raven totem!"

This time the chief called for him to stop but the thief paid no attention.

"Here's the rest of our totem, Pam," Pete said as the girl caught up to them.

"Oh, wonderful! I hope we can find the treasure in it."

In spite of all the years the totem pole had been hidden, the raven's head still was in good condition. Pete turned the pole around and peered at a hole cut into the back of the head.

"Is this where they put the ashes of the dead?" he asked Chief Harris.

"Yes," the officer said as he put his hand gingerly into the opening.

"Is—is something in it?" Pete asked excitedly.

"No. It's empty." The chief withdrew his hand, while Pete exhaled a discouraged sigh. "Farley has the message or the treasure, or whatever was in there," the boy said.

"Then let's catch him!" Pam urged.

Without hesitating a moment, Pete reached for a sapling. Pulling it to the ground, he swung himself up the slope. "I'll get him!" the boy muttered as he climbed around a boulder.

The others hurried after him, but Pete was already out of sight. He felt certain that he was making faster time than Farley. He did not see the cunning fugitive, however.

After ten minutes Pete stopped to listen. There was not a sound in the dense forest except the cry of an eagle wheeling high overhead. Where were the others of his group, he wondered.

The boy put two fingers into his mouth and gave a shrill whistle. No reply.

"Pam! Uncle Russ!" the lad shouted. The dense woods muffled his cries.

Pete sat down on a stump and looked about, bewildered. "Crickets!" he thought. "I'm lost!"

While the boy tried to figure out if he should go on or try to find Pam and the others, his sister, Uncle Russ, and the police chief suddenly noticed that Pete was nowhere in sight.

They called out his name, with no response. Pam's first fear was that Farley had caught her brother, but her uncle doubted this.

"I believe that thief will get away as fast as possible."

"Did Pete have a compass?" Chief Harris asked.

"No."

"More than likely he's lost," the officer remarked. "But when my posse arrives we'll find him."

At that moment the three searchers heard shouts from below them on the hillside.

"That may be Pete now with the posse!" Pam exclaimed jubilantly. "Pete! Pete!" she shouted.

But the answering cries were not from her brother. To everyone's amazement, the oncoming group were Mrs. Hollister, Aunt Marge, and the five other Hollister children.

"This way, Marge!" Uncle Russ sang out, as he

and Pam hastened to meet them. Ricky dashed up with Teddy and Jean, while Holly lagged behind, helping Sue.

"How did you get here?" Uncle Russ asked.

Aunt Marge said that after receiving his message at the hotel, they had hurried to police headquarters. The posse was just setting out and permitted them to come along.

"We followed your broken trail," Mrs. Hollister added, then asked, "Did you find Farley?"

"No, he got away," Uncle Russ said, and Pam told them sorrowfully, "Pete's lost."

"Oh, dear!" Mrs. Hollister looked about nervously. "There are so many wild bears in these woods. I—I hope he didn't meet one!"

Chief Harris said they would continue the search for Pete immediately, then he asked about his posse. Mrs. Hollister said the men had fanned out at the base of the mountain and were gradually pushing up the hillside in the hope of surrounding the fugitive.

"Randy showed us your trail," Jean explained.

Suddenly Holly noticed the raven's head which Uncle Russ held under his arm. Excitement ran high among the children as the story of the missing totem was quickly recounted.

The entire family pushed on until they reached a little clearing. There it was decided that the two women would remain with Holly and Sue while Jean, Teddy, and Ricky joined the others in a search for Pete.

"May Sue and I play with the raven's head?" Holly asked.

"Yes," Uncle Russ replied. "Take care of it until we return. And don't leave this spot."

The searchers felt it would be best to spread out in a long line, each one within earshot of the other. Ricky took a position to the far left. Next to him came Uncle Russ, then Pam, Jean, Teddy, and finally Chief Harris on the right.

"In case of bears," the chief directed, "shout as loudly as you can. They can sometimes be frightened off."

The party advanced, looking right and left and constantly calling Pete's name. By the time they reached the top of a steep ridge, the children were nearly hoarse from shouting. Ricky was about to give a shrill whistle when his gaze fell upon something bright lying beside a patch of ferns. He bent down to pick up a mottled white stone.

"Come see this, everybody!" he yelled. "I think I've found a clue to Pete!"

CHAPTER 17

FACING A BEAR

"PETE must have dropped this pebble," Ricky said excitedly, as he bounced the little white stone up and down in the palm of his hand. "This is the same kind we found at the glacier."

"That's right," Pam said. "If we can find some more, they may show us which direction he took."

A quick and thorough search was made of the area. Teddy found another round stone. Then Chief Harris picked up a third white one.

"Now we're getting somewhere," the officer said, beaming. He ran a finger over his bristly mustache and squinted his eyes. "This shows that Pete turned north here."

His deduction proved to be correct, for as the searchers wheeled left they found more of the white pebbles. They continued to shout and finally they heard a voice, hardly audible, from the trees toward the west.

"Pam! Uncle Russ!"

"Here we are, Pete!" Pam shouted.

"Stay where you are!" Uncle Russ commanded. "We'll be right there!"

"You've found the secret!"

The searchers climbed in the direction of the boy's cries. Finally they came upon him, leaning against a tree, nearly exhausted.

"Crickets!" Pete said, managing a grin. "I thought I'd never get out of these woods!" Then ruefully he added, "I suppose Farley got away."

"I'll leave him to my posse," Chief Harris declared. "Come now. Your mother is waiting." He explained where she and the two younger girls were.

Presently they reached the other Hollisters, who were greatly relieved to see Pete safe and sound. In the midst of the joyful reunion, Sue tugged at Pam's hand. "Our poor raven is hurted."

The black wooden head with the curved beak was nearly too heavy for her to hold up. She thrust it toward her sister. "Look, its nose is coming off."

Pam took the wooden bird. Her smile turned to a look of amazement as she felt the raven's beak. It was loose.

"Look, everybody!" she called excitedly.

Turning the raven's beak back and forth she gradually began pulling it out of the wooden head.

"Yikes!" Ricky cried as the beak came off.

Inside the head was an opening!

Not daring to express her wildest hope, Pam put her hand inside. It touched something crinkly, and she pulled out a folded piece of parchment.

"You've done it, Pam!" Pete cried. "You've found the secret!"

With trembling fingers Pam opened the old parchment.

"Jumping salmon!" the chief said. "It's a map!"

He and the others pressed closer for a good look. Lines were drawn this way and that on the paper. Then, at the end of one line there was a large black X.

"What do you make of it, Chief?" Uncle Russ asked.

"It looks like a mine to me. Look here. These lines must represent the shafts and tunnels."

As the older children eagerly discussed the possibilities, little Sue got tired of standing on her tiptoes. She bent down to pick up the raven's head with its detached beak and walked to one side of the little clearing.

"Poor thing," she said. "Poor humpty-dumpty raven. Don't worry. I'll put you back together again."

Just as the little girl sat down on a mossy spot she heard a noise in the woods and turned to look. Crashing toward her from among the trees was a towering brown bear. Sue was directly in its path!

"Help!" she screamed, as the bear lunged toward her.

At the same instant Pam dashed across the clearing, swept the little girl into her arms, and dashed out of the path of the bear.

The animal continued his headlong rush. But after lumbering into the clearing, he stopped and stood up on his hind legs.

"Yell! Holler! Make all the noise you can!" Chief Harris cried out.

Released from their momentary panic, everyone joined in, making a furious din. The huge bear took a step backward, his beady eyes fixed on the shouting group. Finally, frightened by the commotion, he dropped to his forefeet, turned and disappeared into the woods.

"Thank goodness!" exclaimed Mrs. Hollister, praising Pam for her bravery. "So that's the grizzly the Alaskans talk about."

Suddenly a tiny giggle broke the tension. Sue pointed a finger at her uncle. There stood the cartoonist, pad and pencil in his hands. He had made a sketch of the bear while the others were frightening the brute away.

The police chief shook his head admiringly and said, "You're a brave man!"

When Pete asked the officer why he had not shot the bear, Chief Harris replied that wounding the beast with small bullets would only have infuriated him.

"Do you suppose he was hungry, Daddy?" Jean asked.

Her father laughed. "I don't know about the bear, but I am!" he said, glancing at his watch. "I think we'd better return to Sitka."

"We can show this map to Mr. Gallagher," Pete spoke up eagerly. "Maybe he can figure it out for us."

Chief Harris accompanied them to the shore, saying he would wait for the posse. Because there were so many Hollisters, he suggested making two trips to Sitka in Randy's plane.

Mrs. Hollister, Aunt Marge, and the girls went aboard for the first flight. The pilot returned a short time later to pick up Uncle Russ and the boys. They carried the two pieces of the totem pole onto the plane with them.

At the hotel once more, the Hollisters enjoyed a late but delicious lunch. Sue was so tired that Mrs. Hollister took her upstairs for a nap and remained with the little girl while the others took the map to Mr. Gallagher.

They found him seated in the sun on a bench in front of the Pioneers' Home. When they told him what had happened, the old man pulled a pair of gold-rimmed glasses from his pocket and adjusted them on the bridge of his nose. He studied the map thoughtfully for a few minutes.

"Please, what is it?" Pete begged to know.

"The old mine at Juneau."

"The one on the side of the hill?" asked Teddy.

"Yes. I used to work there," Mr. Gallagher replied.

"What do you think the X means?" Pam queried.

The old sourdough smiled. "I'd venture to guess something is hidden at that point."

Ricky looked glum. "Then we can't look for it. People aren't allowed in the mine any more."

Aunt Marge said that possibly they might obtain special permission.

At this suggestion Pete beamed with anticipation.

"Let's fly back to Juneau on the late plane today! Perhaps we can explore the mine tomorrow."

All but Pam and Jean hurried to the hotel to start packing. The two girls ran to the Kindue home to say good-by.

"Please tell Rossy and Beth," Pam said to Mrs. Kindue, "that we have to leave and we hope they catch a bigger fish than Pete's."

"Thank you, dear," the Indian woman replied. "Do you know that yours is the largest reported so far?"

Thrilled with this news, the girls raced back to the hotel to tell Pete. Then Sue was awakened from her nap. The first thing she asked was whether or not the bad man had been captured.

"No word about him yet," her mother said.

Uncle Russ had made plane reservations and the Hollisters hurried to the seaplane basin. Minutes later they watched the incoming plane skim to a landing.

Soon they were aboard and the craft took off for Juneau. It climbed steeply, gained the summit of the mountains which rimmed Sitka, and set on a slanting beeline for Juneau.

"Yikes!" Ricky exclaimed. "It's like riding a toboggan without touching the snow."

The white-topped peaks gave way to green forests. Finally the pilot cleared a mountain ridge. Ahead lay Juneau on the opposite side of the Gastineau Channel. The pilot cut his motors and glided down through a wedge-shaped valley before landing gracefully on the water.

The Hollisters went straight to their hotel, where Uncle Russ telephoned the mining company.

"If you will make this one exception," the cartoonist told an official, "we may solve an important mystery."

There was a pause. Then he said, "Thank you. Yes. An expert guide would be appreciated. We'll meet Mr. Judson here at ten o'clock."

When Uncle Russ hung up, the children shouted for joy. "I wish tomorrow was right now!" declared Holly.

The Hollisters spent the rest of the day wandering about Juneau. Ricky and Holly liked the flight of wooden stairs which led up the hillside from one street to the other. Pam thought the most beautiful sight was the small streams which cascaded down the sheer rock face of the mountain behind the city.

Next morning there was an excited babble at the breakfast table. Uncle Russ grinned. "I think I'm just as excited as the children."

At ten o'clock the entire family, wearing shirts and dungarees, gathered in the hotel lobby. Presently a small, spry man walked in. The sight of his wrinkled face told the Hollisters he must be at least seventy years old, but he had the springy step of a person much younger.

Seeing the children, the elderly man smiled and his bright blue eyes twinkled. He walked briskly up to Uncle Russ.

"I'm Dynamite Judson," he introduced himself.

Without hesitation Sue spoke up, "What a funny name!"

"Hush!" Mrs. Hollister told her daughter.

"That's all right," Mr. Judson remarked as he patted Sue's head. "I got the name Dynamite because I used to be in charge of blasting operations at a mine in the Yukon territory."

The Hollisters took an instant liking to Mr. Judson and Pete asked, "May we start our trip right away?"

"After I see your map," was the reply.

Uncle Russ, who had taken charge of the parchment, showed it to the old man.

"That's the Juneau mine, all right," he said. "I know exactly where the spot is. But——"

"But what?" Pam asked.

"It might be dangerous there."

"We'll be careful," Ricky said quickly, fearful that Mr. Judson might change his mind.

The elderly man told them that the mine was full of crumbling rocks. "But if we walk carefully, I think we can manage it," he said.

Two taxicabs carried the group along the shore road south of Juneau, then up a steep slope to the mine's entrance. Mr. Judson requested the cab drivers to wait for them, then produced a key from his pocket. He opened a tall gate and the Hollisters followed him inside.

"We'll need lights," said Dynamite. Coming to a little shed, he unlocked the door. Inside he found electric lanterns for the entire party and handed one to each of them.

"Now turn on your lights and then follow me," he directed. "But try not to touch the walls in the tunnels."

Deeper and deeper they walked into the hillside. The entrance, at first large enough to admit a truck, gradually became smaller and smaller.

Mr. Judson stopped to examine the map. "We take a right-hand turn here," he said.

Now the treasure hunters were deep in the old workings. The walls of the tunnel were damp, and a rusted narrow gauge track occasionally glistened from the moisture that had dripped down from the roof of the passageway.

Sue, holding Mrs. Hollister's hand tightly, said, "This is spooky! But I love it!"

"Are these walls solid?" Ricky asked.

Before Mr. Judson had a chance to answer, the boy laid one hand against the spongy rock wall. A few pebbles fell down. These were followed by several chunks of rock that clattered against the old tracks. The sound echoed and re-echoed in the gloomy vault.

Dynamite suddenly called out fearfully, "Run! Hurry!"

CHAPTER 18

A BAG OF NUGGETS

THE Hollisters ducked out of the way just as a large piece of the roof tumbled down with a shattering impact. Particles of dust floated up, making everyone cough and sneeze.

"I—I'm sorry," Ricky said, his voice quavering.

"You made me get all dirty," Sue scolded her brother.

Dynamite said the results might have been worse than that. Flashing his light back, however, he was relieved to find that the rubble in the passageway was not sufficiently high to block their return.

"Please be extra careful from now on," he warned. "The spot marked X is not far from here and we all want to get there in one piece."

With their torches stabbing through the darkness again, the party continued on. Finally Dynamite stopped and pointed to the side of the tunnel.

"Here's the place marked X."

At first nothing unusual was evident to the searchers. They shone their lights around the rock wall, careful not to touch it, lest they set off another landslide.

Then Pam asked, "What's this, Mr. Judson?" She pointed to the end of a spike driven into the wall.

"You have sharp eyes," the miner told her.

Cautiously he put his hand on the spike. It would not budge. He pulled harder. Suddenly the long piece of metal yielded. Dynamite pulled it out and flashed his light inside the small opening.

"Well, I'll be a gold bug!" he exclaimed. "There's a little crypt behind here."

Using the spike as a digging tool, Dynamite carefully chipped away the loose stones.

"Is something inside it?" Pam asked excitedly.

"Yes, there is." The miner tried to reach his hand inside, but the hole was too small. "We can use one of you youngsters for this job," he said.

"I have a small hand," Holly spoke up.

"Good. Reach inside."

Holly put her hand into the hole and her fingers touched a leather sack not much larger than her fist. She pulled it out.

"Hurray! Hurray!" yelled Teddy, jumping up and down. "We've found it! We've found the treasure!"

"Wait. Let's look first," Dynamite advised.

The thong at the neck of the sack had rotted so that it was easily opened. The lights from all the searchers were focused on the find.

Dynamite whistled. "Gold nuggets!"

"I guess that's really the treasure we've been looking for." Uncle Russ grinned.

"There's something inside!"

"And it belongs to us!" Ricky chortled.

"Perhaps someone else has a claim to it," Uncle Russ said.

"Like Ben Roebuck or Emmet Gallagher?" Jean spoke up.

"What did you say?" Mr. Judson was so startled to hear these names that he stared at the Hollisters. "Why, I haven't heard of those fellows in years," he said. "They're old buddies of mine! I thought they had died long ago."

As the little group retreated through the tunnels, Pam told the miner the entire story of their trip.

"By George!" Dynamite exclaimed. "I think I can piece together the rest of the riddle for you."

"Please do!" Pete begged.

Mr. Judson said that many years before, a thief had stolen a pouch of gold nuggets from Mr. Gallagher. He had hidden it in a mine, but nobody knew which mine, nor where.

"Then the thief died."

"With the secret?" Pete asked.

"No. He turned a map of the place over to a renegade friend of his, who secreted it in a totem pole in Haida country."

"That was the totem pole we found yesterday!" Pete declared.

"Right," said Dynamite as they saw daylight at the entrance of the tunnel. "Well," the old miner went on, "after hiding the map in the totem pole, he told the Indians that the totem was jinxed. The chief finally got rid of it but wouldn't tell where the pole was."

Uncle Russ chuckled. "Abalone Farley did us a real favor when he found it."

"Yes," Mrs. Hollister said, adding, "but I would still like to get back the money and other things Farley stole."

When they reached Juneau, the Hollisters thanked Dynamite Judson for his assistance. They went at once for their luggage, then hurried toward the plane to take them back to Sitka so they might return Mr. Gallagher's fortune to him.

They arrived at the old Russian capital just as some of the fishing boats were coming in from the second day of the Derby. Rossy and Beth were on board theirs. When they saw the Hollisters step off the seaplane, they rushed up to greet them.

"Pete, your fish is still the largest catch!" cried Rossy.

Beth smiled. "My brother won a prize yesterday," she said proudly. "He brought in the largest cohoe of the day and received a special reel for a prize."

"Congratulations!" said the Hollisters.

"The police caught Farley, and he still had your money and other things," Beth declared. "They've already been sent to your house in Shoreham."

Everyone rejoiced that the thief had been taken into custody. The next thing was to tell Mr. Gallagher the good news.

With Pam carrying the bag of nuggets, the Hollisters and the Kindue children started off. They found Mr. Gallagher on the lawn of the Pioneers' Home. When he heard their story, he could hardly believe it.

"My nuggets! After all these years!" he exclaimed. "I'll share them with you," he offered.

"No, you mustn't do that," Pam said.

"I don't know how to thank you," the old man went on. His eyes grew moist and he mopped at them with his handkerchief. Then he continued, "Would you please take half of them to Ben Roebuck in Shoreham?"

"We'll be glad to do that," Mrs. Hollister assured him.

Mr. Gallagher counted out the nuggets and divided them, putting twenty of the precious lumps in Mrs. Hollister's hand. "And tell Ben to have some fun with them!" He chuckled.

After Uncle Russ had made a few sketches of the old sourdough, he said, "We'll have to go now, Mr. Gallagher."

The cartoonist said he had made plans to fly from Sitka to Ketchikan, where they would meet his company's airplane. "We'll stay at Ketchikan tonight," he said, "and start back to the States tomorrow morning."

Hearing this, Rossy and Beth looked sad. "I wish you could stay here with us a long, long time," the Indian girl said.

"We'll write to you," Pam promised.

The Hollisters returned to the shore front, where Uncle Russ supervised the loading of their baggage onto another plane.

"Catch me if you Ketchikan!" Ricky shouted impishly as he boarded the aircraft.

"What about the raven's head?" Teddy asked.

"I have it in my suitcase," his father said. "It's my souvenir of Alaska."

After a stopover at Ketchikan that evening, the travelers met the big plane at Annette Island Airport. The pilot was amazed to hear of the children's adventures since he had left them.

By morning the Hollisters were thinking of home as the craft roared nearer and nearer to Shoreham. Suddenly their attention was diverted by a voice over the loudspeaker.

"A special message has just arrived for Pete Hollister," the pilot said. "It reads: 'You have won the Sitka Salmon Derby. Congratulations! Signed Rossy.'"

"Crickets!"

"Yikes!"

"Hurray, hurray!"

Mrs. Hollister held her hands over her ears as the shouts drowned out the sound of the motors. But she beamed proudly at her son.

"You did it!" Pam cried, giving her brother a hug.

"What's the prize?" Ricky asked.

Uncle Russ said he knew the answer to that. "A runabout motorboat," he said.

Pete spoke quickly. "I'm giving it to the Kindue children."

"You're a generous and fine boy,"Aunt Marge said.

"Rossy and Beth deserve it," Pete said. "Without their help I wouldn't have caught the fish at all."

"Shall I send them a radio message to that effect?" Uncle Russ asked.

"Right away!" Pete replied, grinning.

The cartoonist stepped forward to the pilot's cabin and instructed Chet to relay the message.

When the cartoonist returned, he sat down and began to sketch the children's happy faces.

"Wait until we tell our friends about Alaska," Ricky said with a chuckle. "They'll hardly believe us."

Holly rested her chin on her forefinger and said dreamily, "Poor Joey Brill. I hope he's all over his poison ivy by this time."

Just then the captain spoke again. "A return message from Rossy and Beth," he said and read:

" 'Thanks a million for the runabout. Good luck to everybody. Hope Uncle Russ got all the pictures he wanted. We'll see the Happy Hollisters in the funnies!' "